Haunted Is Always in Fashion

Rose Pressey

KENSINGTON PUBLISHING CORP.
http://www.kensingtonbooks.com

KENSINGTON BOOKS are published by

Kensington Publishing Corp.
119 West 40th Street
New York, NY 10018

All Kensington Titles, Imprints, and Distributed Lines are available at special quantity discounts for bulk purchases for sales promotions, premiums, fund-raising, and educational or institutional use. Special book excerpts or customized printings can also be created to fit specific needs. For details, write or phone the office of the Kensington special sales manager: Kensington Publishing Corp., 119 West 40th Street, New York, NY 10018, attn: Special Sales Department, Phone: 1-800-221-2647.

Kensington and the K logo Reg. U.S. Pat & TM Off.

ISBN-13: 978-1-4967-0553-2
ISBN-10: 1-4967-0553-X
First Kensington Mass Market Edition: December 2016

eISBN-13: 978-1-4967-0554-9
eISBN-10: 1-4967-0554-8
First Kensington Electronic Edition: December 2016

10 9 8 7 6 5 4 3 2 1

Printed in the United States of America

To my son, the kindest, most wonderful person I've ever known. He motivates me every day. He's the love of my life.

Chapter 1

Cookie's Savvy Tips for Vintage Shopping

❦

*Adding vintage items
to contemporary pieces in your wardrobe
will add that special flair you're looking for.*

A police car zoomed by with its sirens blaring and lights swirling. Not ten seconds later, another one sped by my red 1948 Buick convertible. Cotton ball clouds drifted like sailboats across the blue sky. The sun popped in and out from behind the clouds, warming up the morning, but the air had shifted. Fall had arrived in Sugar Creek, Georgia . . . not that it would bring a big change. Nonetheless, I loved this time of year.

I had left my house bright and early so that I wouldn't be late for my meeting with Juliana McDaniel. The author had contacted me last week for an interview. She was writing a book about vintage fashion and apparently wanted my expertise. Of course I was flattered that she'd asked. My name is Cookie Chanel and I'm a vintage clothing connoisseur.

Since Juliana had never been to Sugar Creek, I'd decided to meet her at the edge of town at a little café called Sweet Southern Charm. The food was decent, but nothing compared to my friend Dixie Bryant's place, Glorious Grits. I hoped Dixie didn't find out about my trip or she'd think I was cheating on her diner.

I was wearing a pair of 1950s classic white, yellow, and gray checkered plaid knee-length shorts and a white short-sleeved Oscar de la Renta sweater. I'd finished my outfit with a pair of Salvatore Ferragamo navy blue flats. I'd found the sweater at a yard sale for the out-of-this-world price of one dollar. That steal had put me on cloud nine for the rest of the day.

The ghost sitting beside me in the passenger seat had decided to wear Louis Vuitton black slacks and a pale yellow silk Carolina Herrera blouse for our meeting. Yes, I said *ghost*. Although she wasn't into vintage clothing as much as me, she still had impeccable taste.

Charlotte Meadows, the late socialite and businesswoman from Sugar Creek, was now one of my best friends. She was opinioned and stubborn but could be a real doll sometimes too. My best friend Heather Sweet didn't share my opinion of Charlotte. They fought like cats and dogs most of the time. Heather owned an occult shop, Magic Marketplace, right next door to my boutique. She was a non-psychic psychic. More about that later.

"What do you think is happening?" Charlotte leaned forward in the seat for a better view down the road.

I glanced in the rearview mirror and noticed more emergency vehicles. "Whatever it is, it must be serious. I hope everyone is okay."

A little farther ahead, the road was blocked off. No traffic was being allowed through. Police cars had surrounded a black vehicle stopped at the traffic sign. An ambulance whizzed past us.

"Oh, maybe it's a fugitive on the run," Charlotte said with a little too much excitement.

"I certainly hope not."

"Isn't that the detective's car?" Charlotte pointed to a nondescript car on the side of the road.

Detective Dylan Valentine stood beside it, talking with another officer. He'd recently come to the Sugar Creek Police Department from Atlanta. That was something we had in common since I'd lived there for a number of years before deciding to come home and open up the boutique.

Charlotte described Dylan as the cat's meow. She was pretty accurate about that. His six-foot stature had the perfect muscle proportions, his clothing always fit like he'd stepped off the page of a magazine, and he kept his thick dark hair short and cropped. He was wearing tan trousers and a white shirt rolled up to his elbows.

Charlotte tapped on the dashboard to grab my attention. The breeze caused by her motion made the fuzzy dice dangling from my rearview mirror swing from side to side. "You should pull over and see what happened."

Did I mention that Charlotte was persistent and kind of bossy?

Not because she told me to, but because I was a little curious, I decided to check it out. "I suppose I can't get past. Juliana will wonder what happened to me."

"She'll learn that you're always late anyway."

"I am not always late. Just a little rushed, that's all." I steered the car to the side of the road and shoved it into park.

A few cars had lined up on the road, waiting to get through the intersection. I climbed out from behind the wheel and crossed the street.

Just as I made it to the other side, Dylan spotted me and immediately headed my way. "Cookie, what are you doing here?" Concern filled his voice.

"I was supposed to meet someone at the diner down the road." I glanced at my watch. "Looks like I need to call her and let her know I'll be late. Was there an accident?"

"We're not sure what happened yet." His answer was cryptic.

"I hope it's not serious." I craned my neck for a closer look at the black car. "Why are they covering the car with that—" Before I finished the sentence I realized what was going on. The person in the car was dead. I looked back at Dylan.

He gave me a look of understanding.

"The person's a goner. Can't you tell?" Charlotte said with a cluck of her tongue.

Leave it to Charlotte to get right to the point.

"Do you know who it is?" I asked.

Dylan ran his hand through his thick hair. "Not yet . . . a young female."

"That's tragic," I said, almost under my breath.

For a moment we stared in silence. Law enforcement and other emergency workers moved around the scene like a colony of ants. A few other people looked on in curiosity. An officer waved at Dylan, grabbing our attention.

Dylan's blue eyes held a magnetism I couldn't quite put into words. "I'll be back in a minute. Wait for me, okay?"

I wrapped my arms in front of my waist. "Sure. I'll be here." Where else was I going anyway?

"He's so handsome and sweet. You really got a good one with him," Charlotte said dreamily.

"I don't know that I have him." I looked down at my shoes so it wouldn't look as if I was talking to myself. "We'll see where things go."

Dylan and I had gone out a few times and I enjoyed his company. My grandmother Pearl had always told me to be cautious, to never give my heart away too soon. She'd been full of great advice, like never leave home without your red lipstick, pearls, and mascara. Granny Pearl was a Southern woman who never left home without a full face of makeup, white gloves, and hat.

She had been the one who gave me my nickname Cookie. My real name is Cassandra Chanel. Not only did Granny Pearl and I look alike with the same brown hair and eyes, but just like me, fashion was her passion. Her favorite designer was Coco Chanel. So with my love of cookies, the name Cookie seemed like a perfect fit with the last name Chanel. Now everyone called me Cookie.

"She's right, you know. The man is handsome. Are you dating?" a woman asked, breaking into my thoughts.

I looked to my left to see a young blond woman standing next to me in the spot where Dylan had just been. I hadn't seen her approach. Upon further inspection, I noticed she was wearing a cute 1960s white vintage skirt with a little pink floral pattern. If my memory was correct, the designer was Pauline Trigere. The blonde's top was a pretty pale pink, and although not vintage, it matched perfectly with the skirt. I sensed something strange about her though and couldn't quite put my finger on it.

She caught me staring at the skirt, so I had to say something. "Your skirt, it's vintage." I pointed.

She reached down and touched the fabric. "Yes, I love vintage."

"Me too. What a coincidence. I own a vintage clothing store—It's Vintage Y'all—in Sugar Creek." I motioned toward downtown.

The blonde didn't look at me. She was fixated on the scene of the accident, studying every move everyone made. "I was supposed to meet you," she said in a soft voice.

"Oh, you're Juliana. I'm glad that you made it past the traffic." I stuck out my hand. "It's nice to finally meet you."

That explained why she was wearing vintage.

She still didn't take her eyes off the accident, so no handshake. "I'm not sure what happened to me. It happened so fast."

I lowered my hand and quirked an eyebrow. "What do you mean?"

"That's my car." She pointed at the black Toyota surrounded by police.

A small gasp slipped from my lips. *Oh no, not again.*

Chapter 2

Charlotte's Tips for a Fashionable Afterlife

Shopping in the afterlife is fabulous.
If you see something you like,
simply envision it on your body and it's yours.

Charlotte sat in the front seat of my car because she refused to give up her seniority. She always called shotgun. Juliana was too shocked about the fact that she was dead to even care if she sat in the backseat. Charlotte had been in ghost form longer and had come to grips with it. Juliana had not. Like everything Charlotte had done while living, she'd mastered the whole haunting thing. She knew all the details of navigating the spirit world and would show Juliana the ins and outs.

Dylan had said he'd be in touch since he would be on the scene for a while longer. He had no idea I had the victim in the car with me. Obviously, my meeting plans had changed, so I was headed back to my boutique in downtown Sugar Creek with one more ghost than I'd left with.

I peeked in the rearview mirror at Juliana. She stared straight ahead in shock. I was at a loss for words. Even though I'd grown accustomed to being around ghosts, it was still awkward finding just the right words to say. If someone had told me six months ago that I would be communicating with the dead, I would've never believed it. Just walking past the cemetery had creeped me out. Now I was driving around with two ghosts as passengers in my car. It was like I was the shuttle service for the afterlife. Next stop, eternity.

I exchanged a look with Charlotte.

She tossed her hands up as if to say, *I don't know what to do.*

She was supposed to be the expert at this whole death thing. She should know what to do.

"Can I do anything for you?" I directed my question toward Juliana.

She leaned forward and placed her elbows on the back of the leather seat. "This just doesn't make sense. One minute I'm driving along the highway enjoying my favorite Taylor Swift song, and the next minute, I'm dead."

"Did you have an accident? What happened?" I made a right turn.

She plopped back onto the seat. "I knew instantly that I was dead because I was looking at my body in the car. Can you believe it? I was literally standing outside the car, looking at myself. I mean, I've heard about these situations where people die and tell you what it's like when it happened . . . but they go back into their bodies. I stayed out." She threw her hands up. "So here I am. Now what?"

Now what indeed.

"She's a dramatic one, isn't she?" Charlotte rolled her eyes.

Juliana glared at Charlotte. "Who are you?"

Charlotte turned slightly in her seat to eye Juliana up and down with her laserlike focus. "Who am I? Who am I?"

Uh-oh. Charlotte did have a bit of a quick temper.

"I'm the first ghost around here and I will always be first. So don't you forget it." She waved her finger at Juliana.

"Juliana, this is Charlotte Meadows. She's dead too. She was murdered a few months back."

"Please tell her that I was the best businesswoman this side of the Mason-Dixon line." Charlotte tilted her head up.

I smirked. "I think you just told her, Charlotte."

"She just follows you around?" Juliana asked.

"And what do you think you're doing, missy?" Charlotte huffed.

"I just got here. I don't know what I'm doing," Juliana said. "Cookie, you will let me know as soon as the detective tells you what happened to me?"

I steered the car onto Main Street. "Of course, absolutely. I will let you know right away." I had a feeling Juliana would be around to hear the whole thing. I couldn't have two ghosts again. How could I get rid of her? Deep down I knew this ghost wasn't going anywhere anytime soon.

Chapter 3

Cookie's Savvy Vintage Clothing
Shopping Tips

Much vintage clothing is considered timeless
and classic. Therefore, the pieces can be
considered wardrobe essentials.

We parked in front of my boutique. It was a cottage style building that I'd had painted a soft lavender shade with white trim. The big windows on each side of the door were my favorite. They stretched from roof to floor, allowing me to display my clothing to the maximum and, I always hoped, attract more customers. In the display areas, bright colored leaves and pumpkins were scattered around to welcome fall.

In one window, the mannequin wore a deep crimson colored Suzy Perette coat dress. Left unbuttoned, it could be worn as a coat, but buttoned it made a fabulous dress. The mannequin held a black leather

Gucci bag in her hand with black and white Mary Jane pumps on her feet.

The mannequin in the other window featured a 1980s black Dolce and Gabbana silk cocktail dress. Embroidered lace edged the hem of the fabric. Black Dior heels finished the look.

I climbed out of the car and stepped over to the sidewalk. The IT'S VINTAGE Y'ALL sign hung above the entrance.

I'd just reached the front door when Charlotte said, "Here comes trouble."

Heather was headed toward me. She gave tarot card readings in her occult shop and sold just about anything someone would need in order to navigate the paranormal world.

Charlotte and Heather had a strained relationship, but they had made progress to get along. They tended to bicker a lot though. Of course Heather couldn't see or hear Charlotte, so I was stuck being the one in the middle, relaying the snarky messages.

"I thought you had a breakfast meeting," Heather said as she approached. Her dark blond hair was pulled back into a ponytail. She wore a white T-shirt that read IT'S A MYSTICAL THING. YOU WOULDN'T UNDERSTAND. Her designer jeans made her long legs look even more fabulous than they already were.

I shoved the key into the door and unlocked it. "You're not going to believe what happened."

Heather followed me inside. "I don't like the sound of your voice."

I'd dropped my cat Wind Song off at the shop before leaving for the meeting. She meowed and pawed at my leg in greeting. She'd been coming to work with me every day for months, ever since she showed up one day out of the blue. I had no idea how she'd found me.

Wind Song was no ordinary cat. Aside from being beautiful with her long white hair and green eyes, she communicated with me. I know that sounded crazy, but it was a fact.

After flipping the shabby chic WELCOME sign to OPEN, I switched the lights on, and Charlotte and Juliana entered the shop too. I headed across the room, placed my purse on the counter, and released a deep breath.

Charlotte made herself at home on the velvet settee to the right of the counter. Juliana stood in the middle of the room, absorbing her surroundings. She still had that dazed and confused look on her face. I couldn't blame her for that. I wouldn't handle the situation as well as she had.

"There's another one," I said matter-of-factly.

Heather quirked an eyebrow. "Another what?"

I gestured with a tilt of my head. "Another ghost."

Heather slapped her hand on the counter. "Shut up! Why does this keep happening to you? Who is it this time?"

I brushed the hair out of my eyes. "Juliana McDaniel. The woman I was supposed to meet this morning for the interview."

Juliana released a little sigh.

Heather's mouth dropped open and her green eyes bugged out. "She's a ghost?"

I sat on the stool behind the counter. "I'm afraid so."

"How did this happen?" Heather asked.

"That's what I'd like to know," Juliana chimed in.

"We don't know yet. It didn't appear to be an accident. Dylan was on the scene, but he was cryptic about any answers." I picked up a black 1960s sweater with tiny pearl buttons that stretched from the collar to halfway down the front of the garment.

"Don't worry. He'll tell you everything. He can't resist your womanly wiles." Heather wiggled her perfectly sculpted eyebrows.

Charlotte chuckled as she studied her flamingo pink polished fingertips. "Cookie wouldn't know what to do with a womanly wile if it smacked her in the face."

I glared at her for a second then said, "Anyway, Juliana is here now. That's about all I know."

Heather peered around the room as if she'd see Juliana.

I pointed toward the left side of the room. "She's by that mannequin."

"Nice to meet you," Heather yelled.

"She's a ghost. She's not deaf," Charlotte snapped.

Like my Granny Pearl used to say, Charlotte could start an argument in an empty house.

A tiny grin slid across Juliana's face. The first one I'd seen since we'd met. "It's a pleasure to meet you too," she said.

I filled the cat's water and food dishes and placed them back on the floor. "Juliana said the same."

"How will you get rid of her?" Heather whispered.

"She can hear you, dear," Charlotte whispered in Heather's ear.

Heather had no idea that Charlotte was standing so close, but she brushed at her ear as if swatting away a fly.

I moved over behind the counter again and sorted through a few small items I'd left there last night. "I guess we'll find out what's keeping her here."

Juliana glanced over at us. "I didn't choose to be here."

Obviously our discussion wasn't making her feel any better. Maybe it was time for a change of topic. Or at least lighten the current one.

I smiled. "I'm glad you're here."

Charlotte scowled. "You didn't say that when I showed up."

"Well, Charlotte, you can be a bit of a pain in the rear."

Charlotte puffed her chest out. "Well, I never."

"You're glad I'm here?" Juliana scrunched her face in a frown.

Okay, maybe that hadn't come out so well.

"What I mean is, you seem like a nice person and if I'm going to be haunted by someone, I'd pick you. I'm *not* glad you're dead." I picked up a silk scarf.

"Aw, that's so sweet," Heather said.

Juliana perused some of the clothing on the rack next to the counter. "I have to say, Cookie, I didn't know you were so—"

"Crazy?" Charlotte finished the sentence for her.

I tossed the white and blue polka-dot Chanel scarf in Charlotte's direction. "Charlotte, I am not crazy." Of course I hurried over to retrieve it from the floor. No sense in damaging a fine piece of vintage.

Charlotte moved closer to me. "Crazy is nothing to be ashamed of, darling. Remember, we embrace crazy here in the South. We parade our crazy around town and show it off."

I placed my hands on my hips. "That makes me feel so much better. Thank you for the encouraging words."

"What will they do with my car?" Juliana asked.

I tapped my fingers against the counter. "Hmm. I suppose the police will take it for evidence."

Juliana leaned against the counter. "I had quite a few vintage pieces inside. I'd hate for them to get lost or damaged."

"That would be terrible. I can ask the detective about them."

Juliana slumped her shoulders. "I guess I don't need to interview you now."

I wished I could hug her, but my arms would float right through her.

Heather had been listening to my one-sided conversation and moved closer to me. "We could ask the cat if she knows what happened."

I stared at Heather. "We couldn't. Could we?"

She raised an eyebrow. "I don't see why not. We've done it before."

She was right about that. We'd done it quite a few times. I should be used to it. I just wasn't sure if Juliana would want to hear the answer.

"What are you all talking about?" Juliana asked.

"Oh, don't let them scare you. They're just going to have the cat read the tarot cards or use the Ouija board." Charlotte waved her hand. "It's all routine around here. You'll get used to it after a while."

Juliana backed up, moving toward the door as if she wanted to escape. She didn't take her eyes off us.

"It's not as strange as it seems," I said. Okay, it was as strange as it sounded, but I wanted to make her feel better.

Juliana reached the door and turned toward the window.

"Charlotte, you've scared her. Stop doing that," I warned. To Juliana I said, "It's nothing evil or spooky. I don't like scary either. Wind Song uses the letters on the board so she can spell." I tried to let my voice sound breezy and casual, as if luring in a scared cat.

"I'll get the Ouija board." Heather rushed out the door. She had no idea Juliana was there.

Juliana stared out the window. I wasn't sure if I had convinced her yet.

After she realized there was nowhere else to go, she asked, "The cat uses this stuff to communicate with you?"

"Yes, Wind Song just gives us simple answers to questions," I said.

Heather bounced back through the door with the Ouija board under her arm. I still didn't let her keep the thing over at my shop. I had no desire to attract any more spirits than I already had. Wind Song could use the thing and that was it. I didn't want any of the spooky stuff that sometimes accompanied the board.

Charlotte motioned for Juliana to join us at the counter. "Just watch and see."

Juliana glanced over her shoulder one more time and then finally moved to where we'd all gathered around. Wind Song sat on the counter patiently waiting for Heather to place the board in front of her. Once in position, the cat reached out and placed her delicate paw on the board.

Juliana's blue eyes widened. "I can't believe it."

Charlotte leaned against the counter. "Told you."

"It gets better," I said.

Wind Song moved the planchette around the board. She finally stopped on the letter *C*. Heather scribbled the letter onto the notepad. She didn't want to miss a thing. Next Wind Song stopped on the letter *A*.

"Is she spelling *cat*?" Heather whispered.

"She'd better not be asking for more cat food," I said.

Wind Song liked to demand her favorite food. Gourmet tuna was her favorite. The fancy feline glided the planchette over to the letter *R*. After that, she moved on to spell the words *IN* and *THE*.

"Car, in, the?" Heather looked confused.

"In the car," I said.

Without warning, Wind Song jumped off the counter and over to the window to settle into her favorite spot in the sun. Apparently, it was her way of telling us that she was done with her message. She'd gotten the sentence backwards, but I was sure

I knew what she was trying to say. But what did it mean?

"In the car? What car?" Heather looked at Wind Song as if she'd respond.

We looked at each other and said at the same time, "What's in Juliana's car?"

Chapter 4

Charlotte's Tips for a Fashionable Afterlife

❧

*Wearing polyester leisure suits
will send you straight to hell.*

All was quiet in the boutique except for the Big
Band music playing faintly in the background. Everyone seemed to be lost in their own thoughts. As I
straightened racks of clothing, I contemplated all that
had happened. Heather leaned against the counter
tapping her fingers against the wood. When her cell
phone rang, we all jumped at the unexpected noise.
She fumbled around in the bottom of her giant burlap
tote bag until she finally pulled out the phone.

"I expected her to pull out the kitchen sink from
that thing." Charlotte rubbed her temples as if the
noise had actually brought on a headache.

I didn't mean to listen in on Heather's phone call,
but it was kind of hard not to hear.

Heather straightened and her eyes lit up. "Sure,

Cookie closes her shop in just a few minutes and we'll be on our way."

I waved my hands, trying to stop her from talking. I didn't know where she was volunteering me to go, but I was pretty sure it was a bad idea. The last thing I needed was for her to get me into another sticky situation. She was good at that. In spite of my best efforts, she hung up the phone and grinned at me.

"Who was that?" I asked. "And I'm not going."

She looped her bag across her shoulder. "Sure you want to go. That was Fatima. Remember, she's the one with the wonderful psychic abilities I told you about. I met her a few months back at the psychic fair in Atlanta."

Fatima was the woman from Savannah who'd said she might have information about Wind Song. She'd claimed to have seen the cat months before I found her. Unfortunately, the woman hadn't been at her occult shop the day we went, so we needed to return to see if we could find answers to how the cat could use tarot cards and the Ouija board. I wasn't convinced that she knew what she was talking about, however, I wanted to hear what she had to say. Heather was right. I wanted to go.

Proud of herself, she asked, "So are you ready?"

"Just let me close up," I said, knowing I was defeated.

"We're not going to that kooky woman's place again, are we?" Charlotte asked.

I grabbed my purse. "Well, I want to see what she has to say, Charlotte."

Heather placed her hands on her hips. "Is she

complaining about going? You can tell her that she doesn't have to go."

I rolled my eyes. *Oh no, here we go.*

"You tell her that I'll go anywhere I want," Charlotte said, waving her hand in front of Heather's face.

I stood between them. "Ladies, ladies, there's no reason to fight. We'll all take a nice drive and have a pleasant time."

They scoffed in unison, crossing their arms in front of their waists. At least we had a reprieve from the bickering. Even if short-lived.

After locking up, we climbed into the Buick. Heather wasn't about to let Charlotte call shotgun.

We reached Fatima's shop and I parked near the door. I loved landing a prime spot right out front. I could keep an eye on my wheels. Heather and I climbed out of the car with the ghosts following right along behind us.

Charlotte hurried around me. "I still don't see why you need to do this."

"Because I want to find out where Wind Song came from. It's too mysterious that she can use a Ouija board and read tarot cards. There has to be an explanation for that." I pushed the hair out of my eyes.

Heather turned around and scanned the direction where she thought Charlotte would be. Of course Charlotte was on the opposite side, but I didn't tell Heather. It would only frustrate her more. Charlotte smirked, proud of her trick.

"That's a good point, Cookie. We do need to find out where Wind Song came from and this is the perfect place to do that, don't you think? Where else would a supernatural cat come from if not from an occult shop?" Heather moved down the sidewalk as if she was trying to find Charlotte. "I know you're around here somewhere, Charlotte."

Charlotte didn't take her big brown eyes off Heather. However, she didn't offer a comeback, which was totally unlike her. Heather opened the door and I stepped inside first.

The woman waiting at the counter was staring at me. "You must be Cookie Chanel," she said with her raspy voice.

"I am." *The one and only Cookie Chanel with the psychic cat.* "Are you Fatima?" I closed the distance between us.

"That's me." She stretched out her delicate hand, dangling the gold bracelets around her wrists.

I was excited to get right down to the questions and pulled a picture of Wind Song out of my purse. "Thank you for meeting with me today."

She looked at Heather and smiled. "It's nice to see you again."

"Likewise," Heather said in a bashful voice.

I held the photo out to Fatima. Maybe it was my imagination, but it seemed as if she was a bit intimidated. "I thought I'd confirm this was the cat in your shop." Heather had told me that Fatima had wonderful psychic abilities.

She glanced at the photo. "Yes, that's the cat."

"She barely even looked at the photo." Charlotte

tried to take the picture, but her hand went right through it.

I couldn't argue with that. Fatima seemed distant, as if she didn't want to discuss the cat.

"Did you happen to remember any more about Wind Song?" *Do I sound too anxious?*

She pushed up the sleeves on her long white shirt. "Yes, the cat has been in the shop, but I don't know where she came from. One day she just appeared. I gave her food. Right after that was when we did the séance. I can't remember how long ago, but it was several months. The participants for the séance were new customers."

Whether she was telling the truth or not, I couldn't tell, but I had to take her word for it. I honestly just wanted some kind of answers as to where Wind Song possibly got her talent and how she had gotten from Savannah to Sugar Creek. I'd heard stories about pets traveling a long distance, but that was usually to find their owner. "Can you tell us about the séance?" I asked.

"A woman wanted to contact a relative." Fatima's brown eyes shone with kindness.

Okay, that wasn't so unusual. Nothing strange about that. Lots of people wanted to contact a relative through séance.

"Anything special happen?" I pressed.

"The cat appeared."

"Appeared?"

"Yes . . . appeared. It had beautiful white fur and hypnotizing green eyes. She sat nearby as we made contact with a spirit." Fatima's velvety eyes looked as if they were trying to send an unspoken message.

"Who was the spirit?" I asked, curious.

"I've held a number of séances, so it's hard to remember."

How many customers does she have? Apparently she was busy. I searched my brain for questions that might help her recall anything unique about the cat—anything that would stick out in her mind—and came up with only one. "Do you remember who the woman was?"

"I don't remember offhand. Please, I just can't give out the name exactly. You understand . . . confidentiality and all."

Fatima wasn't helping me much. What was I going to do? Even the tiniest clues were better than nothing, I supposed. I pulled a business card from my purse. "Thank you for your help. Here's my card. If you think of anything or remember who your client was, please call me."

She took my card and offered a faint smile. "I'll call you."

I hoped that was true.

"Well, she was as useless as a screen door on a submarine," Charlotte said.

We headed out of the shop. The sky began to deepen toward sunset, giving relief from the warmth of the day. A hint of cooler weather drifted with the clouds coming from the west. Charlotte and Juliana walked beside me as we headed down the sidewalk. I knew Charlotte had more to say.

"I'm just saying I think that she could've given

you a little more information." Charlotte's tone hinted at her frustration with our lack of progress.

"I think she doesn't know anything right now. She'll tell me if she thinks of anything else."

Charlotte adjusted the collar on her yellow blouse. "She probably just wants you to come back and buy something. Or maybe she'll charge for the information."

We reached the car. I unlocked the door for Heather, went around to the driver's side, unlocked and then opened my door. "I don't think Fatima is like that."

"Like what?" Heather slid onto the leather seat.

"Charlotte thinks Fatima will ask for money to give me the information."

Heather rolled her eyes. "Charlotte, you're so cynical."

"I'm a businesswoman and I know how these things work. Plus, I know a charlatan when I see one."

Relaying the message to Heather would only cause more fighting. Their bickering gave me a headache. I shoved the key into the ignition and cranked the engine. The setting sun sent streaks of shades of purple and orange across the blue sky. Fleecy clouds dotted the blue sky as the road stretched before us. We drove back to Sugar Creek with Doris Day's sweet vocals filling the car.

"Do you think a ghost could've entered the cat during the séance?" I asked as I steered around a curve.

Everyone in the car remained silent and just stared at me.

Finally, Heather said, "Yes, I suppose it's possible."

"Anything is possible . . . since that cat can be psychic," Charlotte said from the backseat.

"That's exactly what I thought." *But who was the woman who'd wanted to contact her relative?*

Perhaps we would never find out . . . unless Wind Song wanted to share that with us. We rode in silence for a bit longer.

Suddenly, Juliana leaned forward in the seat. "I just have to know what happened out there on the road. Do you think you could call the detective and ask for any updates?"

She was so polite . . . in stark contrast to how Charlotte demanded answers.

"Cookie, you have to help the poor girl." Charlotte looked at Juliana and said, "You have to *demand* things."

Great. I didn't want Charlotte teaching Juliana her tricks.

Chapter 5

Cookie's Savvy Vintage Clothing Shopping Tips

*A vintage outfit can look modern
by adding a new handbag or shoes.*

I had just pulled the car in front of my shop when my phone rang.

"It's Dylan calling. I know by the smile on your face," Charlotte said.

Okay, she had me on that one. Maybe I was smiling when he called.

"Good evening," he said when I answered. "I have some news about your friend."

"What did you find out?" I asked.

"What's he saying?" Charlotte whispered as if someone might hear her.

Juliana leaned over the seat. "Did he find out about me?"

"Unfortunately, we found out she was shot."

My mouth dropped. "So it wasn't an accident."

Juliana rested her arms on the back of the front seat. "I knew it wasn't an accident."

"This was no accident"—Dylan said—"but you didn't hear it from me. I just thought you should know since you were friends with her."

I hardly knew her, but I wasn't going to correct him on that. "Thanks for letting me know."

"I'll stop by later," he said.

"Well, what happened? What did he say?" Juliana asked as soon as I hung up the phone.

I looked at her in the rearview mirror. "He said you were shot."

She flopped back on the seat. "What a horrible way to go. It wasn't an accident?"

"They don't know that for sure. It could've been a stray bullet."

"Oh come on. What are the odds of that?" Charlotte said.

I looked at her. "I know it would be unlikely." I again looked at Juliana in the rearview mirror. "I mean, who would want to kill you?"

Juliana she shook her head. "I never saw anyone or anything. Why would someone want to kill me? I've never done anything bad. I don't think I have any enemies."

She was a sweet girl and I believed her. Who wouldn't like her? She was always kind. Was she hiding a secret from me?

"Well, I believe that Dylan will find out who did this to you." I pulled the keys from the ignition and opened the car door. As soon as I got to the rear of the car, Juliana and Charlotte were already there waiting for me.

It's Vintage, Y'all stood out from the rest of the historic section, which was made up of old brick buildings. I loved the soft lavender color of my building. I looked into the large windows, proud of the display I'd been redesigning. Okay, I was always changing things up. Since Halloween was quickly approaching, I'd thought to include clothing that could be used as costumes—poodle skirts, bell bottom jeans, and flapper style dresses, just to name a few.

Juliana shook her head. "You can't leave it up to the detective. You have to help me. He has many cases to work and you don't, so you could spend all your time focused on this."

"I wouldn't say all of my time. I do have the boutique." I pointed at the sign dangling above the front door and walked up the sidewalk. I unlocked the door and went inside. Wind Song jumped down from the window sill and greeted us.

The same shade of lavender on the walls complemented the white chairs and crystal chandeliers, giving the inside a glam look. Kind of like old Hollywood.

"Hi, Wind Song. Are you hungry?"

She followed me across the floor toward the counter where I kept the food. With her graceful movements, she reminded me of a Southern belle. Wind Song's gorgeous white fur looked like silk. Her green eyes sparkled like emeralds. Sometimes the way she looked at me made me feel as if I'd known her all my life.

I reached under the counter and pulled out her favorite gourmet food—Shredded Tuna with Greens in a Savory Broth. She'd conveyed that message many times with the Ouija board.

Charlotte stood near the counter, glaring at me. Her cool elegance couldn't hide the frustration on her face.

"What?" I asked.

"Cookie Chanel, you know you have to help this girl. Tell her right now that you're going to help find the murderer."

As difficult as it was, I tried to ignore her. I had so much work to do and it was scary getting involved in another murder investigation. I felt as if I was putting my life on the line. Nevertheless, I knew that I had to help. I couldn't say no. I mean, Juliana needed me. Sure, the police were looking into it, but they could only do so much. Wouldn't a little bit of help from me be a good thing?

Juliana and Charlotte stared at me. When Wind Song finished her food, she focused on me too. She sat on the floor, licking her paws while watching me.

It felt as if she, too, was telling me I should investigate. Finally, I looked at Juliana and said, "Okay, I'll help you."

She finally cracked a smile. "Thank you."

Charlotte flopped down on the settee. "Okay, so where do we start? Who do you think would do this to you, Juliana?"

Juliana looked confused. "I have no idea. I don't think I have any enemies."

"Well, it doesn't take enemies to kill you, honey.

Trust me, I should know. I didn't have any enemies. I mean everyone in town loved me." Charlotte made a wide gesture with her arms.

Laughter overcame me and I held my side.

Charlotte tapped her foot against the floor. "What does that mean?"

I took a few seconds to composed myself. "Well, Charlotte, you were murdered. I'm not sure *everyone* loved you."

"My killer was an unhinged deranged lunatic."

"You have a point there," I said.

"I probably didn't tell you one thing," Juliana said.

"What's that?" Charlotte leaned forward on the settee.

I looked at Juliana for an answer.

"I have an aunt who lives here in Sugar Creek," Juliana said.

"Really?" Charlotte sat up even straighter. "Who's your aunt? I know everyone in town."

Charlotte was right about that. She did know everyone in town.

"Well, her name is Regina. I hadn't talked to her for a long time—since I was young, maybe eleven or twelve. She started calling me recently and we kind of reconnected." Juliana's blond hair moved on her shoulders when she shrugged.

Charlotte pushed to her feet and walked over to where we stood. "Regina? Yes, I do believe I know her. She kept to herself, right? A little strange."

I gave her a hard look. "Charlotte, that's not very nice."

Juliana waved. "It's okay. Regina is strange. Eccentric, I guess you could say."

"Yes, that's the polite way of saying she was headed for a stay at the macadamia ranch," Charlotte said. "One peanut short of having a bowl of mixed nuts . . . if you know what I mean."

"Don't listen to Charlotte," I said. "I suppose we could go talk to her and find out if she knows anything."

Charlotte waved her hand. "It's unlikely."

"Oh, I had a bunch of clothing in the car. I wonder what will happen to it," Juliana said.

Immediately my ears perked up when Juliana mentioned the vintage clothing. I'd hate for anything to happen to them. "What kind of clothing?"

"The kind you like. I want you to have them," Juliana said.

"Thank you, Juliana. That's very kind of you."

"You'll take care of them better than anyone I know."

"I don't know what will happen to them, but I could ask Dylan. I doubt he would let me see anything that was in the car though. Everything's probably evidence."

"You could probably convince him to let you see them." Charlotte shimmied her hips. "See if you can convince him. Just don't do that walking thing where you move your hips. It looks like you need a hip replacement or something."

"Thanks for the info, Charlotte. I'll keep that in mind. I suppose I can give him a call and ask."

Charlotte waved her hands. "No, it has to be done in person. You have to see him and bat your eyes a little bit. You know, flirt with him. You do know how to do that, right?"

"I've seen it on TV," I said.

"You two are funny," Juliana said.

Chapter 6

Charlotte's Tips for a Fashionable Afterlife

Avoid sheer fabric.
If you're already a ghost,
you don't need see-through clothing.

After closing up the shop, we piled into my car and headed across town—a two-minute drive—toward the newly constructed police station. I couldn't believe that I had agreed to check out the vintage items in Juliana's car. Dylan would probably not let me anywhere near any of it.

"I really like your progress. You've become a real go-getter now." Charlotte pumped her fist.

"Thank you, Charlotte."

As she looked at Juliana, Charlotte talked about me as if I wasn't even there. "Cookie's going to be just like me. Well, minus the strangled to death part. She just needed a mentor, that's all. She really was clueless before I came along." She continued chattering away but I wasn't sure Juliana was listening.

I was pretty sure she had other things on her mind. I also thought Charlotte should know Juliana was distracted with finding her murderer.

I parked in the lot and headed toward the main entrance. The ghosts followed me in as I stepped into the lobby.

The young officer behind the information desk looked up and gave me a big smile . . . as if he recognized me. "Are you here to see Detective Valentine?"

I gave a nod. Evidently, word had gotten out that I was seeing Dylan.

"I'll go get him." The officer pushed to his feet and walked toward the back.

When I peeked around the desk I spotted Dylan in the back. Our eyes met in mutual surprise and a huge smile spread across his face. I knew that I had that same reaction. I couldn't help that he gave me butterflies.

"They do make a cute couple, don't you think?" Charlotte asked Juliana.

Juliana grinned, but didn't answer. She was too concerned about finding out who had murdered her to think about my relationship status. I would have felt the same way if I was in her shoes.

Dylan walked over to me, his blue eyes sending a jolt right through me. "What a pleasant surprise. I hope you stopped by to see me." He wore tan pants and a crisp white shirt with a red and blue striped tie.

I supposed the other officers would look at him strangely if he wore vintage to work.

My face lit up. "Of course I did." I was a little embarrassed to tell him that I had another reason for the visit.

He shoved his hands into his pockets. "If I know you, Cookie, you didn't just stop by to say hello."

"Well, Juliana was interested in vintage clothing, so I was wondering if you have any items that had been in her car when you found it." I attempted to sound casual, as if it was no big deal, hoping he didn't think I had vintage on my mind twenty-four seven.

"I'm afraid I can't let you see any of those items, Cookie. You know it's an open investigation."

"The items are just sitting in the room, right? It's not like I would actually touch them. I just want to take a peek." I pinched my index finger and thumb together. "There's nothing wrong with that."

"Don't back down. Push forward until he lets you see them." Charlotte would get me arrested.

He studied my face as if he was seriously contemplating my request.

I crossed my fingers that he would finally give in.

He looked around as if he didn't want anyone to hear what he was about to say, but he couldn't hold back the little smile on his face. "Okay, just a little peek. You can't touch anything."

I shook my head. "No, I would never do that." *Unless he turned his back and I absolutely had to touch something to see it better.*

"I could tell you what I had, but it would be better to see it all in person," Juliana said.

She was right about that. I needed to see the things in person.

Dylan guided me through the door and into the back area of the station. Fluorescent lights flickered overhead. The hallway seemed to stretch on for eternity.

He had no idea that Charlotte and the murder victim were with me. What would he say if he knew they were walking right beside him? Once we got to the end of the hall he opened a door and motioned for me to step inside the room. More fluorescent lights blinked above us. The white walls and floors made the room cold and sterile. Boxes lined the shelves.

"How do you keep up with everything?" I asked.

"Every box has a number." He moved over to a locked area and opened the little door. He pulled out several black storage boxes and set them on the counter. After quickly placing gloves on his hands, he pulled out plastic bags from the box.

I peered down at the items, wishing that I could actually touch them. I should have known how hard it would be to keep my hands to myself and off the clothing. Feeling fabric in my hands and seeing the details up close made my heart go pitty-pat. Vintage was my life. After all, I was the connoisseur of vintage. I had a blog devoted to my passion and I'd gotten quite a large following. So much so, I consulted for movies and television shows.

Inside the box was a hat that looked quite impressive. I needed to find out more about it, but it looked like it was rare. Turquoise blue, it had a beautiful gem brooch on the side that sparkled and dazzled in the light.

"So have you seen all you need to see?" Dylan asked.

"Yes, thank you," I said.

He put the items back in the boxes and then put the boxes back on the shelf.

"She had some great stuff in there," I said as he guided me out of the room.

He locked the door behind us. "You really are into your stuff."

"I suppose you could say I have a passion for fashion." I chuckled. *If he knew what I was really up to . . .*

Charlotte groaned at my attempt at humor.

Dylan led me back to the main lobby. "Can I call you later?" He touched my hand.

His sweet tone made a smile spread on my face. "I'd like that."

"I told you they make a cute couple," Charlotte said.

Finally, Juliana had to answer. "Yes, they're sweet together."

With Charlotte and Juliana beside me, we exited the building into the parking lot. As we walked toward the car, Charlotte took the opportunity to tell Juliana about her main squeeze Sam, a ghost I'd helped out not long ago. Charlotte was totally smitten with him. He still popped in and out from the other dimension. Actually, both ghosts had the ability. I had no idea how that supernatural power worked. Apparently, it was something they couldn't tell the living.

When we climbed into the car Charlotte was describing his bedroom eyes.

"Where to now?" Juliana leaned forward from the backseat.

Home sounded like a good idea to me . . . maybe make it a movie night. *Casablanca* was on the classic movie channel.

"We could visit her aunt," Charlotte said.

I tapped my fingers against the steering wheel. "I'm way too tired for that, but we can go tomorrow. Do you think your aunt knows what happened to you?" *I'd hate to be the first one to tell her.*

"I think she probably does," Juliana said.

I spent the evening watching the movie and writing a couple of blog posts about vintage wedding dresses and staying current with vintage clothing. Dylan called and I refrained from asking him more about the case. I figured he didn't want to discuss work after a long day. Tomorrow on the other hand . . . would be a perfect time to ask again.

Chapter 7

Cookie's Savvy Tips for Vintage Shopping

*One piece of vintage can be a focal point
of your outfit. Consider a scarf, hat, or skirt.*

"Aunt Regina lives on Maple Grove Court. Turn left here," Juliana instructed the next morning.

I pulled up in front of a yellow Victorian with black shutters and a black door. A white porch lined the front of the house. "It's a beautiful place," I said, shoving the car into park.

"She inherited it from her grandmother," Juliana said.

Nerves had taken over my stomach at the thought of talking to Aunt Regina. How would she react? I walked up the steps and onto the porch. A white cat ran past and meowed. For a moment, I thought it was Wind Song and almost tripped to avoid it. Regaining my balance and my composure, I rang the doorbell.

The woman who answered the door was probably

five-foot-two—my height. She had short brown hair and big floppy curls that fell around her face. She wore a navy blue floral dress that looked more like a robe. Opening the door wide, she stared at me with her big brown eyes. "What do you want?"

The visit started off badly. *Be polite,* I reminded myself.

I moved back a couple steps in case I needed to leave quickly. "I'm here to see Regina." At her nod, I said, "Your niece Juliana was a friend of mine."

She continued to glare at me.

"I'm sorry for your loss."

She looked me up and down. "Thank you. But what do you want?"

Before I had a chance to answer, a blur of fur ran behind her. She let out a screech, took off running through the living room, and leapt onto the sofa.

I exchanged a look with the ghosts. "What do you think's wrong with her?"

"She's nuttier than a fruitcake." Charlotte looked at Juliana. "Sorry."

I was surprised that Charlotte had even apologized.

"She was always a bit eccentric," Juliana said.

It looked like it was more than a bit, but I wasn't going to mention that.

The fuzzy thing ran by again. It was a squirrel . . . on the loose in her house and having a blast running in circles. More than likely he was just looking for a way to get out.

"Don't just stand out there. Help me get rid of this creature," Regina yelled.

Was she seriously going to attempt to catch it?

I eased into the house, wondering what I was supposed to do. I didn't want the thing to bite me. "I can't catch it."

"I just want it out of here." Regina picked up the broom and swung it through the air.

The only hope we had was to lure the little creature out the open door. I couldn't believe I was helping get rid of a squirrel. As I ran around the living room, the squirrel raced in circles. My only hope was that I wasn't bitten. The squirrel ran up the curtains right behind Regina. She screamed and dashed across the room, hiding behind the recliner. I hoped that the squirrel didn't jump on her back. She'd probably have a heart attack.

"I would have paid good money to see this, and I'm getting to watch for free." Charlotte stood in the corner with her arms crossed in front of her chest.

Juliana stood nearby.

This was no laughing matter . . . until it was over. Then it might seem pretty funny. Okay, a lot funny, actually.

"Oh, for heaven's sake. Do I have to do everything?" Charlotte said in a huff. "I'll get rid of the squirrel." She rushed over to the furry guest and waved her arms in front of him.

I could have done that. How did she think that would possibly help?

Regina had no idea a ghost was trying to get rid of the squirrel.

"Shoo, shoo." Charlotte continued waving her hands frantically.

Regina was still running in circles like she was on a

race track and couldn't get off. Lucky for her, the
squirrel was no longer chasing her. Somehow Charlotte had gotten it close enough to the door to usher the
squirrel out, and I slammed the door shut.

"How did you do that?" Regina asked breathlessly.
She'd finally stopped running.

"Tell her the ghost did it." Charlotte laughed.

"Tell her to sit down and relax," Juliana said.

Thank goodness things had settled down. I hurried
over to Regina and steered her to the sofa. "Everything is fine now."

She plopped down on the sofa and released a deep
breath. "That was a close one. Would you be a doll and
get me some iced tea? I have a pitcher in the fridge."

"One iced tea coming up," I said and then headed
for the kitchen.

"She acts as if it's the first time she's seen a
wild animal," Charlotte said as she followed along
behind me.

Juliana stayed behind with her aunt.

The kitchen was a tiny space—just enough room
for a small table and two chairs. Oak cabinets and
white appliances were set off to the left. I pulled out
a glass from the cabinet and then grabbed the tea
from the refrigerator.

"Be nice, Charlotte. You never know when a
squirrel could bite." I poured the tea.

"If you say so." She leaned against the counter.
"Regina seems dramatic." Charlotte sure was calling
the kettle black.

With the glass in hand, I hurried back to the living

room so that maybe I could finally get some answers. I handed Regina the iced tea.

She looked at the glass. "You didn't add much ice."

"This woman is pushing her luck. I'd give her ice cubes," Charlotte said.

"She's just eccentric, that's all," Juliana said.

"There's eccentric and there's crazy." Up near her temple, Charlotte made a whirling motion with her index finger.

"Would you like me to add more?" I asked.

Regina waved her hand. "No, I'll drink it." She took a sip but didn't look pleased.

"Do you mind if I have a seat?" I gestured.

She waved toward the chair. "Please."

"You have a lovely place." I eased down in the large brown upholstered chair.

She kept her eyes focused on me. As soon as I was settled, she said, "Why are you here again?"

I glanced at Juliana. "Like I said, I'm here about your niece Juliana. I'm Cookie Chanel. I own the vintage shop."

Regina looked down. "It's a tragedy."

"I'm sorry for your loss," I said again. Somehow it felt wrong for me to be there. Juliana's family needed time to grieve without me poking around asking questions.

Regina shook her head. "Of course I haven't seen her since she was a child. She was a precious little one. Always well-behaved and kind."

Juliana preened a bit. "I was a good kid."

"Modest, aren't you?" Charlotte said as she paced around the room.

"I bet you were a brat when you were a kid." Juliana smirked.

Secretly proud of Juliana for standing up to her, Charlotte grinned.

I wasn't sure how to ask the next question. I supposed there was no easy way. If I was going to do it, I just needed to spit it out. The faster I asked, the quicker I could get out of there. I rushed my words. "Do know why anyone would want her dead?"

Regina fixed her stare on me instantly.

I debated whether I should run out the door.

"Like I said, I haven't seen her in a long time. She called recently and told me she would be coming to town. She was going to come and see me."

Juliana sat beside her aunt on the sofa. "I was going to do that. Too bad she doesn't know I'm here."

I wanted to tell Regina that Juliana was sitting beside her, but I didn't want to scare her. Plus, she'd probably think I was crazy and making it up.

"Don't tell her I'm here. It would just scare her," Juliana said as if reading my mind.

"Okay, so she doesn't know anything. We should get out of here." Charlotte motioned toward the door.

I supposed she was right.

"Thank you, Regina. I've taken up enough of your time." I pushed to my feet and headed for the door.

"One thing I'd like to ask you," Regina said as she followed along behind me.

At the door, I turned to face her. "Yes?"

"Juliana mentioned a hat. She was going to give me a vintage hat." Regina twirled the glass as if reminding me of the scarce ice. "You said you have the vintage shop in town. Well, I just wondered if she told you anything about the hat. I'd like to have it as soon as possible. The hat is turquoise with a big brooch on the side."

A flash of the contents in the police station box came to mind. I'd seen a hat in the box, but I had no idea if it was the same one. Regina looked a bit odd.

"You know that the hat would be part of evidence now, right? Even if the police released it, I don't think they would give it to me. Not unless Juliana had instructed for it to be given to a specific person."

"Cookie, do you know what you're talking about?" Charlotte asked.

Of course I didn't know for sure. Charlotte should know that. But it seemed like a logical answer.

"I didn't have a will," Juliana said. "I figured I was too young. Not to mention, I don't have any stuff that's worth anything."

Regina seemed adamant that she must have the hat. Of course, I had to know what was so special about that particular piece. Juliana had not indicated why the hat would have any special meaning.

"I'll make sure to let you know if I find out any-thing about the hat." I inched out the door and onto the porch.

"Thank you. You're a sweet woman." Regina patted my hand.

"Have a good day."

"Cookie is a dear. A little stubborn at times, but sweet," Charlotte said.

Charlotte thought *I* was the stubborn one? She

was the ghost who refused to move on from this dimension.

She walked beside me as we left the house. When I didn't see Juliana, I looked back.

Still beside her Aunt Regina, Juliana tried touching her aunt's arm, but her hand went right through. Regina frowned and looked in Juliana's direction. Apparently, she'd sensed the touch.

She turned her attention to me, and I waved so she wouldn't think anything strange. Juliana finally caught up with us.

I turned away from Regina and talked with Juliana and Charlotte. "It might not be easy, but I'll try to find the hat for your aunt."

Juliana shook her head. "I honestly have no idea what she's talking about. I never told her I would give her a hat."

"What do you think about what she said?" Charlotte asked as we walked to the car.

"What do you mean?" Juliana asked. "She didn't say anything."

"About wanting the hat. That's kind of odd, don't you think?"

"I told you she's always been eccentric," Juliana said.

"Yes, well, you know my response to that." Charlotte whirled her index finger again.

I opened the car door and slipped behind the wheel. "Don't bicker. It gives me a headache. Plus, we have a murder to solve. There's no time for arguing."

"You're right, Cookie," Charlotte said from the passenger seat.

"I'm just so glad you're helping me," Juliana said, leaning forward from the middle of the backseat. "So what do we do now?"

I started the car and pulled away from the curb. Juliana and Charlotte looked at me expectantly. They always expected me to have the answers.

"I need a little time to think about that."

Chapter 8

Charlotte's Tips for a Fashionable Afterlife

*There's no need for dressing rooms
in the afterlife.*

All the way to the shop, Charlotte tapped her fingers against the seat in rhythm to Elvis singing "All Shook Up" on the radio. Of course I had the *all Elvis all the time* station.

I'd been in a hurry to get to Regina's but had managed to put together what I thought was a great outfit. I'd even decided to wear a hat. It was black with a pink flower on the side. My dress was a 1940s black full skirt with dropped waist and a bodice that closed down the front with rhinestones. Sheer fabric covered the satin bottom half of the dress. Tiny black bows were sewn onto the side of the sleeves. I loved the puffy texture of the dress. My shoes were black platform wedge heels. They had open toes with sling back heels and side buckles.

After parking in front of the shop, I hurried out of the car. I loved the attention my car caught when it was parked along the curb. It drew people's eyes to the sign above my shop's door. The shiny red paint was like a giant arrow pointing people into my store. At least I hoped it brought in business.

It felt good to be back at the store. Being surrounded by my vintage finds made me feel safe and peaceful. I unlocked the door and flipped over the sign. As soon as I switched on the lights, Wind Song hopped up to the window ledge where she kept an eye on the Sugar Creek residents. She seemed particularly fond of the fifties pink party dress—designed by Oleg Cassini—in the window. She kept pawing at it.

I had to admit I thought the dress was absolutely divine too. The sleeveless beauty had a full skirt with a pleated waistline. Chiffon draped over the back of the shoulders. It allowed for many different ways for the dress to be worn. I'd displayed it with a petticoat to emphasize the full skirt and paired it with three inch, pink velvet sling back, peep-toe pumps. A tiny bow accented the top of the heels. They were to die for.

"Are you ready for breakfast, Wind Song?" I asked.

She meowed and hurried along beside me. After filling her dishes, I turned on the computer. I planned to research Juliana's hat right away. I wondered why Aunt Regina was so interested in it. In the police station, I'd gotten a quick glance at the hat and hoped I could find a similar one online. I was almost sure

I knew the designer. Research was my favorite kind of detective work. I tapped on the keys.

"What are you doing?" Charlotte asked as she peeked at the screen.

"Searching for the hat." I scrolled down the page.

Juliana was at the front of the store looking out the window. I had a feeling she was thinking about her killer, trying to figure out who had done her in. That was something we all wanted to know.

I scrolled the pictures of hats until I found one that looked similar and clicked on the link. "Ah-ha."

Juliana looked my way, but after a few seconds she turned and looked back through the window.

"This hat is worth thousands of dollars." I pointed to the computer screen.

"Let me see that." Charlotte leaned in for a closer look.

Would that be reason enough for someone to kill Juliana? If so, no wonder Aunt Regina wanted the hat. Would her own aunt kill her for the hat?

A man walked into the shop and immediately started sorting through the rack of clothing on the left. He hadn't looked at the back of the store to notice me. Wind Song jumped from her spot at the window and moved so fast across the room that if I hadn't known better, I would have thought a ghost was chasing her. But Charlotte and Juliana were next to me. Wind Song stared right at the man.

"She's acting strange," Charlotte said. "Well, strange for her, I mean. She is a psychic cat."

For heaven's sake, if I'd known a short time ago what craziness I'd become involved in, I wouldn't have believed it. I moved around the counter to help my customer instead of staring at him as if he was from another planet. Juliana and Charlotte were behind me, but Wind Song stayed on the counter, preferring to watch from a distance.

"He's probably looking for a dress for his girl-friend," Charlotte said.

The man was tall with dark hair. A small beard covered his chin and small portion of his cheeks. He finally glanced up when I approached. As I got closer to him, Wind Song meowed as if warning me to be careful. She'd never done that before.

"Welcome to It's Vintage Y'all. May I help you find something?" I asked.

He smiled immediately. "Good afternoon. I didn't know anyone was in the store."

Charlotte stood next to me, eying him up and down. "Ask him what he wants," she pushed.

I was glad he couldn't see her and I gave her a *look* when he glanced at the clothing rack for a brief second. Unfortunately, he caught me in the act.

Knowing it would be hard to explain, I pretended nothing had happened. I hoped he'd forget.

"Way to chase customers away by making them think you're weird, Cookie."

As if it wasn't her fault it happened in the first place.

I turned back to the customer. "Are you looking for something for your mother? Sister? Girlfriend?" I had the feeling he was looking for something specific.

Charlotte and Juliana stood next to me, waiting for him to answer.

He glanced around the room. "Do you have hats?"

Charlotte gasped. I was lucky I'd been able to keep myself from making the same sound. This was too weird. What a coincidence that he would be interested in hats too.

I stared at him entirely too long. I had to answer. "Yes, I have a few. They're right over here." I moved toward the rack that displayed the hats.

He followed me over to the area. Charlotte and Juliana fell into stride beside us.

"Is there a certain style of hat you're looking for?"

If he only knew the way Charlotte and Juliana were eyeing him. I was sure my expression matched theirs. As he peered down at the hats, Charlotte and I exchanged a look.

After a couple seconds, the man looked up at me. "Are these the only ones you have?"

"I believe so. I may have a few in the back that I haven't gone through yet."

His eyes widened. "Would you be able to do that now?"

I really wanted to accommodate my customers, but I had no one to look after the store while I dug through boxes. "I'm sorry, but they are in boxes. I'd be happy to take a look the first chance I get and give you a call . . . if you could tell me what style you're looking for."

Charlotte and Juliana leaned in closer, as if they would hear better that way. They were already as close as they could get.

The man scowled. "Are you sure you can't look now?"

"He must really want a hat," Charlotte said.

I motioned across the room. "I don't have anyone to watch the store. I promise to call as soon as I can."

"I could watch the store for you," he said.

"I knew this guy was crazy," Charlotte said.

"I'm sorry I can't do that," I said.

He stared at me for a moment and my heart beat a little faster. He was beginning to creep me out.

Finally, he said, "Sure, I understand. My name's Victor Patrick, by the way. I'll write down my number and you can call me."

"That will work. Yes, I'll call you."

"I would lose his number if I were you, Cookie." Charlotte tapped her fingers against the counter.

"I agree," Juliana added.

That might be the first thing they'd agreed on since meeting. I moved toward the counter to grab a notepad and pen.

"I wouldn't turn my back on him, Cookie," Charlotte said.

He seemed a little weird, but I wasn't sure I was ready to label him a serial killer just yet. After all, he'd only asked for a hat.

I wrote his name on the paper and then peered up at him. "What's your number?" After giving it to me, I asked, "You didn't tell me exactly what kind of hat you're looking for."

"I can't wait to hear this," Charlotte added.

"He can't possibly be looking for the same hat," Juliana said.

"So trusting and naïve," Charlotte said. "You'll learn soon enough."

He shrugged. "I guess I'll know it when I see it."

"There's something strange about this guy." Charlotte said that about everyone. She walked around him, looking him up and down.

We watched him walk out the door.

I'd have to find out who he was. At least I had his name. I'd do a quick search and see what I could find.

Wind Song pawed at my arm.

"What's wrong, Wind Song? You couldn't possibly want more food."

She meowed loudly and looked at the door. I knew instantly what she wanted.

Chapter 9

Cookie's Savvy Tips for Vintage Shopping

*Buying vintage jewelry can be
an inexpensive way to start
a vintage collection.*

I picked up the phone and dialed.

Heather answered on the first ring. "What's up?"

"Bring the Ouija board," I said.

"You really need to keep a Ouija board over there so you don't have to borrow mine."

"You know you want to see what the cat has to say too."

She was silent for a moment. "I'll be there in two seconds."

Heather wanted me to get a Ouija board, but I was still holding onto the notion that maybe bad spirits would slip through just by having it in my place. If she wanted one in her shop that was her choice.

It was longer than two seconds, but not by much. Heather's blond hair was braided to one side. Wearing a long blue skirt and a white tank top, she'd gone for the whimsical look. When she was around my mother, everyone always thought Heather was her daughter. They discussed incense and herbs. I preferred to discuss fabric and the cut of a dress.

Wind Song meowed and leapt onto the counter as soon as she saw Heather. It still amazed me how smart the cat was, almost as if there was a human stuck in there.

"Does Wind Song have a message for you?" Heather asked as she placed the board onto the counter.

The cat positioned her body in front of it right away.

"A strange man was just in here and I know Wind Song didn't like him." I stroked the cat's head.

Heather quirked and eyebrow. "Interesting. What did he want?"

I quirked an eyebrow. "A hat."

Heather stared for a moment. "Is that it?"

With no patience at all, Charlotte said, "You'll have to explain it to her or this could take all day. I don't have that kind of time."

"Charlotte, you have all the time it the world," I said.

She huffed. "Never mind."

I explained to Heather. "Juliana's aunt wanted a hat that was in Juliana's car. I just think it's strange that someone else would ask about a hat."

Wind Song placed her pretty paw onto the planchette

and moved it across the board. It had taken awhile, but I was kind of getting used to seeing that.

"What's she doing?" Juliana asked.

"The cat gives messages through the board," Charlotte said as she leaned against the counter.

Juliana laughed. When we didn't return the laughter, she said, "You're serious?"

"Would she really make up nonsense like that?" Charlotte asked.

Juliana sighed. "No, I suppose not."

Wind Song stopped on the letter *H*. Next, she moved to the letter *A* and then on to the letter *T*. She licked her paws, giving the signal that she was finished with the message.

"Hat," Heather said.

"Great. Heather can spell," Charlotte said.

The word lingered in the air.

Wind Song hadn't even been there when Regina mentioned the hat. Perhaps she'd been paying attention to the conversation around the shop after all.

"What about the hat, Wind Song?" I asked. "You have to tell us more."

I already knew there was something going on with a hat, but I needed to know what it meant. Wind Song listened to me and started moving the planchette again. We watched with bated breath as she went from letter to letter. Heather wrote down the message on her notepad as if she was Wind Song's assistant.

When the cat finally stopped, Heather said, "Find the hat."

I blew the hair out of my eyes. "How will I find the hat?"

"The one that the police have?" Heather asked.

"Yes. It will be hard to get them to release that hat to me."

"It won't be hard," Charlotte said.

"Oh, yeah?" I asked.

"It'll be impossible." Charlotte tossed her hands up.

I gave her *the look*. "Thanks for making me feel better, Charlotte."

"Honey, I'm just being honest with you." Her accent dripped with honey.

"How does the cat know this?" Juliana asked.

"What are they saying?" Heather asked.

I explained the conversation.

"We don't know where Wind Song came from, but we're trying to figure it out." I rubbed the cat's head. She purred and then rubbed against my hand.

I might not be able to get the hat, but I'd have to find out what was so important about it. Regina had mentioned it, the cat and a stranger were asking for a hat. That had to mean something.

"Is it just because the hat is valuable?" Juliana asked.

Charlotte played with Wind Song. "It's not worth that much. Not enough for someone to ask about it like that."

"Charlotte's right. There has to be more to it than money." I peered down at the Ouija board.

Charlotte brushed the bangs out of her eyes. "You'd be surprised what people will do for money. And not much of it either."

"We'll figure it out, Cookie. Don't worry," Heather said.

Chapter 10

Charlotte's Tips for a Fashionable Afterlife

*Shopping for sale items
is no longer needed either.*

After coming home from work and cooking dinner of citrus glazed chicken and homemade biscuits, I decided to spend the evening researching the hat. Honestly, I wasn't even sure where to start. How many had been made? What was so special about it? I'd looked everywhere on the Internet and still hadn't found exactly what I was looking for.

"When are you going to give up on finding that hat?" Charlotte was a little shocked at how much I had researched the hat.

"When I find the answer," I said, pulling a book out from the old trunk in my bedroom. "You should know that by now."

"I appreciate all the help," Juliana put in.

"She wasn't nearly as helpful with finding my

killer. I had to push and push." Charlotte's brow furrowed.

"I've gotten a lot better at my detective work now," I said as I walked back into the living room.

"Lucky for Juliana."

I plopped down in the oversized chair. All the research hadn't gotten me anywhere. I tried not to become discouraged. If the book didn't help, I'd just have to think of something else.

Flipping through the book, I held out little hope that I would find what I was looking for.

It was getting late and I only had a few pages left. I knew I'd be disappointed, but I needed to get to bed anyway. I flipped the next page and screamed.

Charlottes screamed and clutched her chest. "Oh my stars, what is it? Why are you screaming like that?"

I tapped the page. "It's the hat."

Charlotte and Juliana rushed over.

"I don't believe that. You can't be serious," Charlotte said.

"See for yourself." I held the book up, pointing to the hat.

Juliana leaned closer. "It's the hat. The exact one."

I must admit I was pretty proud of my accomplishment. I hadn't given up.

"What does it say about the hat?" Charlotte asked.

I tapped the page. "This book was printed in 2006 and I bet it's worth even more money now."

"How much is it worth?" Juliana asked.

"Well, it was one thousand back then. I bet it's up to two thousand now."

"What makes that hat so special?" Charlotte asked.

"What makes this hat special is the designer. The site I looked at earlier had it wrong." I knew my teasing tone would get to Charlotte.

Charlotte leaned closer. "Who's the designer?"

I knew that would interest her. "The hat is Hermès."

Charlotte gasped. "Wow. Hermès."

"I thought you'd appreciate that."

Charlotte paced around the room as I stared at the book. "Cookie, it's great what you did."

"Thank you," I said.

She held up her hand. "Let me finish."

I should've known there would be more.

"The hat is only worth a couple thousand. I think you're hinting that Juliana was murdered for the hat."

"Way to burst my bubble, Charlotte," I said.

She waved her hand. "I'm only speaking the truth. You have to look at all the facts."

"Well, Victor and"—I looked over at Juliana— "Regina were asking about the hat. That seems odd."

"Regina wouldn't want to murder me," Juliana said.

I felt bad for implying that her aunt would do something like that. The harsh reality was that sometimes the one who supposedly loved the victim was actually the murderer.

"Sometimes it happens," Charlotte said.

"You're completely right," Juliana said.

Would that be reason enough for someone to kill Juliana? Would her own aunt kill her for the hat? Hadn't anyone witnessed the murder?

The doorbell rang and we all looked at each other.

"Who could be here this late at night?" Charlotte asked.

That spoke volumes about my social life.

"Maybe it's Heather," Juliana said.

Wind Song jumped off the sofa and raced to the front door. She did that for only one person.

My heart beat a little faster at the thought. "I must look a mess," I said as I tried to smooth down my hair.

Charlotte quirked an eyebrow. I hurried over to the door. It was too dark to see without switching on the light. When I flooded the porch with the light, Dylan's face was looking back at me.

When I opened the door, he was standing in front of me.

"Wow, I didn't expect to see you." I was already in my jammies. The pink ones with the bunnies on them. Dylan was wearing vintage.

"Well, doesn't he know the way to your heart." Charlotte smirked.

"That's about the sweetest thing I've ever seen. He's a dreamboat," Juliana said. "Did I use that word correctly? That's what they used to say, right?"

Charlotte laughed. "Yes, that's what they said."

Wearing the brown pants and white shirt that he'd bought from my shop, Dylan stepped into the living room and looked around. Wind Song jumped up and ran over to him as if she hadn't seen him in years. She weaved around his legs and purred.

"I think she likes you," I said.

"What's not to like?" Charlotte said.

"What brings you by tonight?" I caught myself twisting a strand of hair around my finger like a teenager with a crush. I stopped, hoping that he hadn't noticed.

"Did I disturb you? I should have called first," Dylan said.

"No, I wasn't busy." I glanced over at my laptop.

Charlotte chuckled. "You got that right."

"I'm glad you came by." I really meant that.

"Don't just stand there, offer the young man a refreshment." Charlotte held her hand up to her forehead as if she might faint. "I swear I have to do everything."

"Would you like to have a seat?" I gestured.

"Actually, I had something else in mind."

"Oh, maybe we should leave the room," Charlotte said.

The next thing I knew, Charlotte and Juliana had vanished. He moved over to the table and placed his phone down. Music came from the tiny speaker. It was loud enough for us though. "Moonlight Serenade" by Glen Miller filled the room.

Dylan held his hand out to me. "May I have this dance?"

The smile on my face was instantaneous. "Yes, you may."

He pulled me close to his body.

Charlotte and Juliana peeked around the corner. Charlotte gave a thumbs up and then they disappeared again. Dylan's cologne was intoxicating. My body was next to his as we swayed back and forth to the music.

"You're a good dancer," I said.

Dylan smiled a little sheepishly. "I had to take ballroom dancing in college. It was the only class I could get in and I needed the credit."

I laughed. "Well, it worked out well for you."

His body felt perfect pressed next to mine. I rested my head on his chest and soon became lost in the moment. When the music stopped, I had to force myself to move away. Dylan didn't act as if he was in a hurry to move either. Silence filled the air for a moment.

I decided to speak first. "Oh, I forgot to tell you about someone who came into my shop today."

Dylan quirked an eyebrow. "Was there a problem?"

"Well . . . not exactly."

"That doesn't sound good." His eyebrows furrowed.

"He just acted strange, I guess. He asked about a hat." My voice was full of suspicion.

Dylan studied my face for a moment. "And that's a bad thing?"

I chuckled. "Okay, that sounds crazy, but it's just that Juliana's aunt Regina had asked about a hat too. I thought it was an odd coincidence that someone would come in and ask for the same kind of hat.

Especially the kind of hat that was in the murder victim's possession."

"Tell him the hat is in the box at the police station and you want it," Charlotte said from the kitchen.

I knew they had been listening.

"So what did you find out about this man?" Dylan asked.

"I got his name. Victor Patrick."

Dylan looked a little surprised that I had found out that much. He really shouldn't have been shocked.

"I'll see what I can find out about the man. In the meantime, we shouldn't talk about the case tonight."

"He's right. It's not romantic," Charlotte yelled from the other room.

I wanted to yell back that her interruptions and eavesdropping weren't romantic either. I figured she was selectively remembering that. Juliana was quiet and let Charlotte do the talking. If I could just get Charlotte to be quiet too . . .

Dylan walked back to his phone and turned the music back on. "How High the Moon" was one of my favorite songs.

"I didn't know you knew so much about old music," I said as we swayed back and forth.

"I'm learning," Dylan said with a smile.

"Isn't that the sweetest thing?" Charlotte added.

Just then his phone rang, cutting off the music and breaking up our dance.

Dylan paused and then said, "I guess I should answer that."

I really didn't want him to but said, "It could be important."

He answered the call. By the sound of his responses, I knew it wasn't a good one. He had the strangest look on his face when he turned around.

Chapter 11

Cookie's Savvy Tips for Vintage Shopping

*Vintage fashion will make
your wardrobe unique. No one else
will have your one of a kind piece.*

"I don't like the sound of this." Charlotte peeked around the kitchen doorway.

"What happened?" I asked.

"I have to go." Dylan stuffed his phone into his pocket. "I'm sorry, Cookie."

That didn't answer my question. "That's okay. I understand if you need to go."

He ran his hand through his hair. "No, it's more than that."

Charlotte and Juliana reappeared in the room. I knew Charlotte wouldn't want to miss out on this.

His gaze didn't leave mine. "Someone broke into your shop."

My heart sank.

"What?" Charlotte's voice echoed around the room.

Dylan touched my arms. "Try not to worry. I'll call you as soon as I find out anything. I'm going there now." He rushed out the door, leaving me confused and upset.

"You know what you have to do, don't you?" Charlotte asked.

"I know exactly what we're doing. We're not staying here." I grabbed my keys. "Come on. Let's go."

"See, I like the way she thinks," Charlotte said to Juliana as we rushed out to my car.

I cranked the engine. The fuzzy dice hanging from my rearview mirror swayed as I hurried out the driveway.

"Dylan can't possibly think you'll stay put when something has happened to the shop," Charlotte said from her usual spot in the passenger seat.

"What do you think happened? Who could do this?" Juliana asked as she leaned forward from the backseat.

"I hope they catch the spineless lizard who did this." Charlotte pumped her fist.

"If anyone can, I think Dylan will," I said.

I made it to the shop in record time. I figured all the police would be there so I wouldn't get a speeding ticket. Plus, I had a good excuse for punching the gas. My father would be upset if he'd known I was driving recklessly. He said to never go more than five miles per hour over the speed limit. Under the circumstances, I figured six was a safe number.

Quite a few police cars were parked in front of the

shop. That made it so much more real. I had hoped it was just a false alarm.

I parked the car as near the shop as I could and hopped out. Charlotte and Juliana were slightly in front of me. They didn't want to wait and moved a lot faster than me. I rushed up to the store. An officer tried to stop me.

"I own the shop." I pointed to it.

Dylan spotted me and rushed over. "Cookie, what are you doing here?"

"You didn't think I'd stay behind, did you?"

"I didn't want you to be injured if someone was still here."

My eyes widened. "Is the burglar still here?" I looked over his shoulder into the shop.

Several officers stood around, but it didn't look as if anyone was in danger.

"Everything is okay now. Your alarm was tripped. The door was open."

"How did they get in?"

"That's what we'll try to figure out. We'll check for prints."

"Is anything missing?" I asked.

"You can come in and tell us if anything looks out of place." Dylan ushered me into the shop.

"This is terrible. Why has crime come to Sugar Creek?" Charlotte asked.

"It's everywhere, Charlotte," I said.

"Did you say something?" Dylan asked.

Oops. "I was just talking about the break-in."

"What about the surveillance?" Dylan asked.

"I can check that now," I said, moving to the back of the store.

As I passed the hat display, I noticed that they were missing. "Some of the hats are gone."

Charlotte gasped.

"This is bad," Juliana said.

I pointed to where they'd been. "It's not a coincidence that the man was asking about hats and now they're gone."

"We have a hat burglar," Charlotte said with complete seriousness.

"Why would someone take only some of the hats?" I wondered aloud.

"Are you sure?" Dylan asked.

"When it comes to my inventory, I have a photographic memory."

Dylan called an officer over and instructed him to do a search on Victor. I hated to get someone in trouble if they had absolutely nothing to do with the break-in. Better safe than sorry though. I moved to get the surveillance device I'd recently added after some strange events had occurred. It recorded everything in the store.

When I reached the door to the back room, I realized that it was open. "I left this door closed."

"The officers have already been back here," Dylan said.

"Oh right." I stepped inside the tiny space and knew right away that the thief had been back there. "The equipment is gone." I pointed to the empty spot on the table.

"The surveillance is gone?" Dylan asked.

I nodded. "All gone."

Dylan checked the room. "This just doesn't make sense, Cookie."

"Maybe they wanted the money," I said.

"You don't keep any money here at night, do you?" he asked.

"No way. But I guess they thought something was here."

"I think it's the hats," Charlotte said.

She was probably right. I was thinking that too, but it just didn't sound reasonable. One thing was for sure—no way was I getting any sleep tonight. What if the person broke into my house? What if I was home at the time?

Dylan touched my arm. "Don't worry. We'll figure this out."

"I'm calling to get someone to change the locks right away." I called a friend of my father's. Any time I needed maintenance help, Clark was right there. His wife had passed away several years ago and he was always trying to stay busy.

I was definitely upgrading my surveillance video tomorrow. I wanted something that would let me check in on the shop from my smartphone. If the technology was there, I needed to use it.

Luckily, Dylan stayed with me until the locks were changed then followed me home. He checked the house while I waited by the door. I was pretty sure no one had gotten in while I was gone, but that didn't mean I wasn't scared that someone would show up in the middle of the night.

"Call me if you need anything," Dylan said.

"I will."

Dylan gestured. "And lock the door."

I felt so cared for. "Always."

He leaned down and kissed me. I was all too aware of Charlotte and Juliana standing behind me in the foyer. Dylan stepped off the porch and got into his cruiser. I closed the door and flipped on the porch light. If anyone was lurking around, I wanted to be able to see them.

"And it had started as such a romantic evening. Maybe you can pick back up where you left off," Charlotte said.

I peered out the door. "With any luck."

Chapter 12

Charlotte's Tips for a Fashionable Afterlife

Avoid the outfit you were wearing when you died.
It will only bring back bad memories.

Ken Harrison walked through the door of the shop the next morning. His blue eyes lit up when he smiled. His blond hair was styled in a short cut. The little bit sticking up in the front gave a slight mischievousness to his otherwise conservative style. As usual, he looked dashing in his blue suit, white and navy pinstriped shirt, and pale yellow tie.

We actually had on almost matching outfits. My pencil skirt was navy blue with white pinstripes. I wore a white blouse with a boat neckline and fitted through the waist. I had a red rose clip in my hair and nude-colored, closed toe stilettos on my feet. My hair was styled with victory rolls and my lips were covered with crimson red lipstick.

"Well, look what the cat dragged in," Charlotte said. "Cookie, his eyes said Va-va-voom when he saw you."

She made me blush.

Wind Song meowed as if to say she had nothing to do with bringing Ken to the shop. He was an attorney in town. We'd sparked a friendship over one of the most morbid things possible—murder. He'd defended someone recently who had been accused of murder. In addition, he was definitely one of the most eligible bachelors in Sugar Creek.

I was about to introduce him to Juliana, but then I remembered he couldn't see her. When I could see her so well and speak with her, it was hard to remember others couldn't. One day I was going to get myself into trouble with that.

"Good morning, Cookie." Ken reached down and rubbed Wind Song's back.

"What brings you by this morning?" I asked.

"Look at the big smile on her face when she sees him," Charlotte said.

Juliana agreed. "He is handsome."

"I wanted to come by and see you anyway, but I also had some news that I thought you might be interested in."

"Oh yeah? What?" I asked.

Charlotte moved closer. "Oh, this sounds juicy." She loved gossip.

"I know you knew the woman who was recently murdered."

I cast a look toward Juliana. She moved over to the counter and looked at Ken.

"Her Aunt Regina has retained me as her attorney, but I don't know why."

"That is interesting," Charlotte said.

"Aunt Regina always was an odd one," Juliana said.

I thought this was a little bit more than odd. "She hasn't been named as a suspect so why would she need an attorney?"

Ken shrugged. "I don't know. I tried to convince her otherwise, but she insists. I don't think there will be any need for my services."

"Well, I guess it's no harm. If she really doesn't need you, you won't have to do anything."

"You should look into this, Cookie. Something's wrong." Suspicion filled Charlotte's voice.

"What are you saying about my aunt?" Juliana narrowed her eyes.

I didn't want the two of them arguing.

"I found one thing curious," Ken said.

Charlotte and Juliana were hanging onto his every word. I suppose I was anxious with anticipation also.

"She's insistent that I help her get the items that were in Juliana's car. She said there were some vintage items that should rightfully go to Juliana's heir."

Juliana shook her head. "It's not like I was a princess or something. The clothes aren't worth much."

"The hat," Charlotte said with a click of her tongue.

"Is there something wrong?" Ken asked.

I was hesitant to say anything because maybe it was nothing. I guessed Charlotte picked up on that.

"You have to tell him, Cookie. Tell him now." She pounded the counter, but her hand went straight through. Of course it made absolutely no noise. She was a master at ghostly activity, but when she was upset, sometimes she couldn't control herself and went back to her old ways. Then her hands flew through walls and everything else.

"I feel like you're not telling me everything," Ken said.

Finally I said, "I went to see Regina."

His eyes widened. "Why would you do that?"

"Well, I wanted to ask her more about Juliana."

"Because you're trying to solve this?" Ken asked.

"Someone has to help Juliana." Without thinking I motioned toward her.

Ken followed my gesture and then frowned. "This is true, but maybe you should leave it to the police."

The topic of the police was something he didn't mention often. He knew I was seeing Dylan.

"Sometimes they need a little help," I said.

Always happy when the police needed a little help, Ken smiled at that.

"Regina was interested in a hat . . . and it was more than just a little interest. Not just something mentioned in passing. She seemed like she wanted a particular hat. She even asked for it."

He didn't understand. "Why would she do that?"

"I think the hat is worth some money."

"So you think she knew about the hat before the murder?" he asked.

I shrugged. "Maybe so."

Juliana waved her hands so I'd pay attention. "That's not possible. I never told her about the hat."

Even Ken seemed a little suspicious of Regina's motives.

"I don't even want to hear about this," Juliana said as she walked away from the counter.

"Go ahead and continue talking to Ken about this, Cookie. Maybe you two can figure it out. It doesn't hurt that you get to look at his handsome face in the process." Charlotte wiggled her eyebrows.

She was always trying to push me into a date.

"I'll see what I can find out," Ken said. "I'll let you know."

"I'd like that. Thank you."

"That's not the only reason I stopped by," Ken said.

"Oh, do tell." Charlotte propped her elbows on the counter and rested her chin in her hands.

I didn't look over at her. Best not to encourage her.

"Is there something else you need?" I asked.

"As a matter fact, I came here for shopping."

"That's sweet," Charlotte said.

I couldn't hold back a smile. "Shopping? This is a treat." I was a bit surprised Dylan had bought some stuff and now Ken too. I'd have the whole town dressed in vintage. "Sure, why don't you pick out an outfit?" I said with the wave of my hand.

"You're the one with the style. I'd love to see what you pick out." Ken touched a necklace on the display near the counter.

Charlotte studied her red fingernails. "He's just

doing this because he saw Dylan wearing vintage clothing."

Not necessarily, I thought. *Then again, maybe Charlotte is right.*

I motioned for Ken to follow me. "I have some great new shirts over here that I think you'll like."

"Put him in royal blue. I think it will look great with his eyes." Charlotte winked.

He would look good in that color.

"Don't you think he has sexy eyes?" Charlotte asked Juliana.

"He's gorgeous," Juliana said. She had been so quiet.

I knew the transition was tough on her. I wished I could do more to help. Finding her killer was all that I could do.

I pulled a blue and white striped cotton shirt off the rack. "Do you like this one? It's from the fifties."

Ken held the shirt up to his chest. "You know I've been thinking maybe you could come with me and speak with Regina. Convince her that the items really aren't necessary for her to worry so much about."

"I'm not sure if she'd want to hear that from me, but I can definitely go."

"Great. I'll set up something and give you a call."

"That doesn't sound like a very good date to me," Charlotte said.

I'd have to remind her that it didn't sound like a date because it wasn't a date.

After I rang up his purchases, he handed me his credit card and flashed his gorgeous big smile at me.

"I'll call you soon, Cookie." He turned and left the shop, a happy customer.

Wind Song meowed as if saying good-bye. Or maybe it was because she didn't want him to leave.

Charlotte was leaning against the counter. "I really like that guy, but I don't know what will come of this meeting with Regina."

"It'll be interesting," Juliana said.

She should know.

Chapter 13

Cookie's Savvy Tips for Vintage Shopping

~~~

Look for great vintage patterns.
Floral, stripes, paisley, and polka dots
are all must-haves for any vintage wardrobe.

I wasn't convinced I could say anything to persuade Regina that Ken's counsel was unnecessary, but he was picking me up and taking me to her house. She was probably just freaked out because the police had been talking to her. Whenever the cops on television came around to talk to someone, that person always seemed to need an attorney. Maybe that's why Regina thought she needed one too.

Honestly, I'd done nothing wrong and I was a little scared too.

Later that day, I closed up the shop and waited on the sidewalk for Ken. Charlotte and Juliana stood with me.

I looked at my watch. "I hope he's not late."

"Well, it's not exactly like you have anywhere else to go," Charlotte said.

"Thank you for that observation, Charlotte."

"I think it's kind of a waste anyway," Juliana said.

I spotted Ken's car coming down the street. "Ladies, try not to get me in trouble, okay?"

Charlotte laughed. "As if."

He pulled up to the sidewalk and hopped out. In a black suit, white shirt, and a red tie, it looked as if he'd just come from the courthouse. "I hope I didn't keep you waiting long." He opened the car door for me and I slid in.

"He's such a gentleman," Charlotte said from the backseat, "but he could stand to get a bigger car." Her Louis Vuitton handbag rested on her lap.

She was a ghost. Why did she need a purse?

Ken pulled away from the curb. "I want to thank you again for coming with me today."

"It's no problem. I just hope that I can convince her."

We made the next right and headed away from town. Within a few minutes, we were turning onto Maple Grove Court.

Ken pulled up to Regina's house and shoved the car into park. "Fingers crossed."

"I hope she doesn't have an escaped squirrel this time," Charlotte said.

We got out and headed up the path to her front door. It felt as if someone was watching me, but when I peered around no one was there. Not even neighbors were outside. Ken rang the doorbell and we waited. After a couple seconds, I thought Regina wasn't going to answer, but then the door opened. She stood in front of us in a black dress and a big black hat.

"Is she going to a funeral?" Charlotte asked.

I exchanged a look with her and we realized it had to be Juliana's funeral. Perhaps we could've picked a better time to visit.

"I hope we're not intruding," I said.

Regina narrowed her eyes and looked at me. "I remember you."

"Yes, we spoke previously. I'm Cookie. I'm friends with Ken." I gestured toward him.

"Hello again, Regina." He gave a short dip of his head.

She stared at me for a moment longer and then said, "Would you like to come inside?"

We stepped inside the house. Luckily no squirrel followed us. Ken never left my side. It was as if he was a little afraid of Regina.

"Why did you say you were here again?" she asked.

"She really has the hospitality thing down," Charlotte said sarcastically.

"Well, you're no flower yourself," Juliana said.

Regina looked at Ken. "Now that you're here, can I get you to help me hang a picture?"

Ken exchanged a look with me. "Sure. Where is it?"

"It's right back here in the bedroom." She motioned for him to follow.

He grimaced and followed her down the dark hallway.

"I have to hand it to her. She gets what she wants."

Charlotte peered out the living room window at the house next door.

"I told you she's eccentric," Juliana said.

I was standing in the living room with the ghosts. I didn't know what to do while I waited. I could have had a seat on the sofa. Then again, I liked staying close to the door in case I wanted to get out of there quickly.

Charlotte turned to face me. "Cookie, you should have a look around while she's gone."

"I can't do that."

"Sure you can. She won't know," Charlotte said with a wave of her hand.

"It's probably not a good idea," Juliana said.

Charlotte looked unhappy with that answer. She tossed up her hands. "You never want to do anything. This isn't even slightly dangerous."

"That's nonsense," I whispered. "Because of you, I'm always doing things that could get me into trouble."

Charlotte placed her hands are hips. "Name one."

"Name one? I can name twenty and they just happened last week."

"Oh, you just want to argue with me," Charlotte said.

"Trust me, arguing is the last thing I want to do."

"You're wasting time while you could be looking." Charlotte crossed her arms in front of her chest.

I gave up. "Okay, okay. I'll look, but it has to be fast. Besides, I don't think I'll find anything."

"I'll keep guard by the bedroom," Juliana said.

"For once she has a good idea," Charlotte said.

I didn't really know where to start. The table by the front door looked like it had a few bills on top. "I suppose I can start over there," I whispered.

I moved closer to the table, but Charlotte stopped me. "You should look in that coat closet first."

I took her suggestion and grabbed the knob. After a brief pause, I twisted it and eased the door open just a little.

"What do you think you're going to find in there? A body?" Juliana asked.

"There could be skeletons in her closet," I said.

"Just hurry and open the door."

Releasing a deep breath, I opened it and saw hats. Lots and lots of hats.

"Wow, she really likes hats," Charlotte said. "Where do you think she got them?"

"I suppose she's been collecting them for a long time."

A lot of the hats were beautiful . . . ones I'd like more time to look at, but I didn't want Regina to catch me.

"I suppose that rules her out as a suspect. Now we know why she was asking for the hat." Charlotte placed her hands on her hips.

"Does it? This could be why she wanted to kill Juliana . . . so she could get that hat."

"True. It might be *the one* to finish her collection." Charlotte tapped her index finger against her lip.

I closed the door. "I don't think she'll ever be finished with her collection."

"Don't forget to look at the table." Charlotte pointed to the one by the front door.

I moved over and started sorting through the envelopes, but nothing caught my eye . . . until I saw the name *Victor*. It was written on a piece of paper along with the name *Hunter*. Who was Hunter? Their phone numbers were also listed. I pulled out my phone and took a quick picture of it in case I needed the numbers for later.

I turned to Charlotte. "Why would she have Victor's phone number?" I said.

Charlotte shrugged. "I suppose to help them plot the murder."

"So you think they were in on it together?"

"What else can we think?" Charlotte said.

I'd just put my phone back in my pocket when noise came from the other room. I didn't want Regina and Ken to catch me snooping so I hurried back into the living room. I spotted a man walking into the kitchen. It definitely wasn't Ken. Surprised, I said, "I didn't know she had a guest."

"I wonder if he heard you talking about Regina being the murderer? He probably thinks you were talking to yourself."

"That would be bad."

He had been in the next room so he could've easily overheard. I hurried over to the kitchen and peeked into the room as the man walked out the back door. He wore all black. I saw only the back side of him but could tell that he had dark hair too.

"That's odd," Charlotte said.

I heard Ken and Regina talking and knew they were headed back into the living room.

Juliana appeared by the kitchen door. "They're coming."

I rushed over and leaned against the chair by the fireplace, trying to pretend that I'd been there the whole time. Did I have *suspicious* written on my face?

"We're innocent until proven guilty," Charlotte said.

Regina narrowed her eyes when she looked at me. "Oh, I forgot you were here."

It was pretty obvious that she didn't like me much.

"I just saw someone in your kitchen, Regina. Did you know you had a guest?"

She had a funny expression on her face for a second and then she said, "Yes, he's a friend of mine."

"Regina has a boyfriend?" Juliana said.

"He must like cranky," Charlotte said.

"Anyway, Regina, back to the reason we're here," Ken said.

"Would you like some iced tea?" she asked.

"Now she's friendly," Charlotte said. "She's just trying to stall and change the subject."

"No, thank you," I said.

Ken shook his head. "No thanks, but back to the reason we're here, Regina. You do understand that there's really no need for my services." He looked at me so that I could talk to her.

"Yes, the police are not going to arrest you." I wasn't so confident when I said that. Maybe she really did need an attorney.

"Well, it's better safe than sorry," Regina said.

"She has a point," Charlotte said. "I always kept an attorney."

How should I ask her about the hats? "I'd like to ask one thing."

"You sure you don't want tea?" Regina said.

"Drink the tea!" Charlotte said.

"I was looking for the bathroom and accidentally opened the closet door."

"Nice try, Cookie, but I don't think she believes you," Charlotte said.

Juliana was staring at me.

Regina narrowed her eyes. She knew where I was going with my question.

"That's quite a collection of hats you have," I said. "Where did you get them?"

She glared at me. "I collected them for a long time. They're all mine."

"She didn't say they weren't yours," Charlotte said.

Regina immediately changed the subject. "If I can't get the hat Juliana had back from the police, I'll be forced to sue them. That's why I need your services, Mr. Harrison."

"I'm afraid I can't help you with that, Regina."

She was clearly angry. "Well, I'll just have to find someone who can."

"That's probably for the best," Ken said. "We'll show ourselves out."

"Fine," she said.

Ken and I walked over to the door.

"I really think you're making a mistake," Regina called after us.

"I think it's for the best," Ken said.

We stepped outside, leaving Regina inside muttering to herself.

"That went just about how I suspected," Juliana said.

"Do you think I upset her?" Ken asked.

"I just think she's upset, that's all. Things will work out. Don't worry." Of course, I didn't know if they would work out for the good or the bad.

We climbed into the car and I looked back at the house. Regina was at the window, but when she noticed me, she moved back and closed the shade.

"Did you really see someone in the house?" Ken asked.

"Yes, he went out the back door," I said as I buckled my seatbelt.

"I get a bad feeling from this," Juliana said. "Maybe we shouldn't leave."

"You think she's okay?" I asked. "Should we help her?"

"I don't think there's anything we can do . . . especially anything that she would allow." He started the car.

"Perhaps there's another family member who could check in on her," I said.

"Maybe, but she lost contact with everyone a number of years back," Juliana said. "Like I said—"

"She's eccentric." Charlotte finished for her.

As Ken pulled away from the curb, I looked out

the back window. A cat that looked exactly like Wind Song sat on the sidewalk.

How could she get there all the way from the shop? I remembered seeing a cat the other day when I visited Regina. Maybe it was that one.

I decided to find out. "You have to stop the car," I said to Ken. "I think my cat is out there."

"How is that possible?" Charlotte said.

Ken pulled into the next driveway and turned the car around. The cat was still sitting on the sidewalk.

I knew right away that it was Wind Song.

"I can't believe it, but that really is your cat," Juliana said.

"How did your cat get here?" Ken asked.

"That's what I'd like to know," I said.

When we pulled up to the curb the cat didn't move. I'd expected that she might run when she saw me. Maybe she didn't want to be caught. She looked at me though. Recently I'd noticed that she didn't want me leaving her, but I wasn't sure why. I suppose I was going to have to start taking her with me more often.

I climbed out of the car. "Wind Song, what are you doing out here?"

She meowed loudly when I picked her up.

I hugged her. "You scared me. Don't ever do that again." I climbed back into the car and sat with her on my lap.

"Maybe the cat just doesn't want you to leave her anymore," Charlotte said.

"How do you think the cat got over here?" Ken asked.

"I have no explanation for that."

"I wish she could tell us," he said.

It was one of the strangest things. Regina's house was simply too far for Wind Song to have walked there in the time we'd been gone. I intended to find out the answers. She was going to answer with the Ouija board or the tarot cards. I didn't care which.

The cat remained on my lap, looking out the window the entire ride back, and even started to purr.

We reached my shop and went inside. I showed Ken the picture of the phone numbers. "What do you think about that? Do you think that one of these guys thinks that Regina has the hat?" I massaged my temples. "It's just so confusing."

"I don't know what to think," Ken said.

Juliana was at the front window staring out again. I knew she was upset by the latest development.

Chapter 14

Charlotte's Tips for a Fashionable Afterlife

*Check fashion shows and magazines,
envision the garment you like,
and you can have the latest styles instantly.*

Ken left and I went right back to work, pricing inventory and putting things out on display.

He'd been gone only a short time when Juliana approached me with a worried look on her face. "Cookie, I have a strange request."

"What's that?" I asked.

"I want to go to my funeral."

I stopped in my tracks. Charlotte was speechless.

"Okay . . . can I ask why you want to do that? It could be traumatic."

"I already know I'm dead," she said.

"Yes, but your friends and family will be crying."

"I'm prepared for that. Sometimes the killer shows up at the funeral."

"Oh, I've seen that in the movies," Charlotte said.

"You know, you're right," I said. "I've seen that too." It also sounded like something the cops would do, and as strange as it seemed, I agreed to take Juliana to her memorial service.

I changed into the simple black skirt and blouse I kept at the shop for emergencies, put on my black heels, and headed out for the car. Charlotte had on her complete funeral attire—hat, gloves, and the whole shebang. Juliana was a little more subtle, but she still wore black slacks and a blouse. She was going to her own funeral!

We arrived at the funeral home and I found a parking spot.

"Looks like a nice turnout," Charlotte said.

Juliana put her hands on her hips. "What did you expect? I have a lot of friends and family."

"Now you get to see who cries over you," Charlotte said.

I gave Charlotte *the look. Knock it off.*

"What? It's the truth," she said.

Inside, the funeral home was quiet except for soft music in the background. Never a pleasant experience to step into one of those places, sometimes it had to be done. Juliana's body had been cremated. I hadn't asked her if that was a choice she'd expressed before she died or if the decision had been made for her after she'd died.

Note to self—make out a will. Charlotte had been on me about that, but I kept putting it off. I was young. Why did I need one? However, look what had happened to Juliana.

"Recognize anyone?" I asked Juliana.

"There had better be someone she knows or this is just plain weird," Charlotte said.

Juliana pointed across the room. "They are my parents. I can't stand to look at them, so we'll just avoid them."

"Okay, but don't you want to talk to your parents?" I asked.

Exasperated, Charlotte said, "Duh. She can't talk to them, Cookie. She's dead."

"Charlotte, you're so sassy," I whispered from behind a giant plant in the corner of the room.

"People might not see you talking to us, but they're still going to think you're strange if they find you hiding back there. Get out here and talk to people," Charlotte said.

"Fine," I said as I straightened my blouse and came out from behind the plant.

Juliana pointed at a couple young women. "There's my friend Trisha. She's cool. Go stand by her. She's talking to another friend, Amy."

I had no idea how I would approach those people. Would I really talk to them? They didn't know me. I was getting a few strange looks which made me feel uneasy. Did they know something about me after all?

"I just can't believe she's gone," Trisha said.

"It's all so unreal." Amy wiped her eyes with a tissue.

"Have you heard anything about the killer?" Tricia asked.

"I heard it was over money," Amy whispered.

"Money?" Juliana scoffed. "I'm dirt poor. Where would I have any money?"

They didn't mention anything else about the murder, changing the subject to the upcoming sale at Nordstrom.

"So much for friends," Juliana said.

"Life goes on, Juliana. Life goes on," Charlotte said.

"Look there's Hunter." Juliana waved. She put her arm down when she realized what she'd done. "Well, we can go stand beside him and hear what he has to say."

"I take it you know Hunter," I said.

"It's called eavesdropping. I suppose that's neither here nor there," Charlotte said.

I stood near enough to Hunter to hear any conversation, but far enough so that he wouldn't notice me. At first, he was alone and looking a little lost. Then another man approached.

Juliana recognized him. "Oh, that's Cooper. They've been friends for a long time."

After their initial chitchat, they changed the subject to Juliana's murder.

"This is what I want to hear," Charlotte said.

"Yeah, the police have been asking me a lot of questions," Hunter said.

"Tell them you don't know anything. Stay strong, man. Don't let them get you." Cooper patted Hunter on the back.

"What does that mean?" Juliana asked.

The conversation broke up so it was possible we would never find out.

I glanced across the room and spotted Aunt Regina. "There she is," I said out of the corner of my mouth, hoping no one would notice me speaking.

Without saying another word, we headed over in her direction. Of course I had to find out what she might say.

"She's talking to my cousin Jasmine."

When we neared, I heard Regina say, "I just love the hat and all I wanted was for them to give it to me."

"Mercy me, she's talking about the hat again. Give it a rest, woman," Charlotte said.

Aunt Regina had a one track mind and kept talking about the hat.

"Oh my stars," Charlotte said.

"What?" I asked.

She pointed and I followed her direction. Dylan was there.

I forgot that the police would really show up. "How will I explain my visit?"

"You're friends with Juliana. Of course you would come. Just calm down. Don't panic."

It was too late for that. I was already hiding behind that plant again.

"It's a little more obvious to be hiding back here, Cookie," Charlotte said.

I couldn't see how it would be obvious. I was totally hidden. I didn't think anyone could see me. Maybe I could just hide until the service started and then sneak out without anyone the wiser.

"Whatever plan you have twirling in that little brain of yours isn't going to work," Charlotte said.

"I'm going to assume that that wasn't an insult, Charlotte." I pushed one of the branches out of my face.

"Assume away. Cookie, I love you, but you have to come out from behind the plant."

"I love you too, Charlotte, but no can do. I'm staying put."

Someone cleared their throat from behind me. I spun around, almost knocking the plant over.

Dylan was standing there with his arms crossed in front of his chest. "Cookie, I guess you have a good explanation for why you're standing behind a plant."

No, not really. I quickly came up with something halfway plausible. "Is this a ficus?" I asked, touching the leaf.

Charlotte practically fell to the floor. "I'm so glad that I'm a ghost and he can't see me. Cookie, please. You're killing me all over again."

Juliana was actually laughing. I had caused her to laugh at her own funeral—quite an accomplishment a lot of people couldn't claim.

Obviously that question didn't work. He stared at me. "You're not here for the plants."

I stood a little straighter. "All right. To be honest with you, I'm not here for the plants."

"Please don't say you're here for the food. Please don't say you're here for the food." Charlotte crossed her fingers.

"I came to see if the murderer showed up."

Charlotte smacked her head. "Cookie, what are you

doing? Why did you tell him that? You're just here for Juliana. That would've made much more sense."

Oh yeah. That would've worked better. Too late. "I suppose that's why you're here too?" I asked.

Dylan bit back a smile, trying not to laugh at me. "Yes, that's why I'm here. So you found out anything?"

"Thank goodness he isn't mad after that crazy explanation," Charlotte said.

"Juliana's friend Amy said she thought the motive might be money. Hunter said the police have been questioning him a lot. Cooper said for him to hang in there and not give into the pressure."

Dylan looked at me. "Wow, that's a lot of information. I didn't know you knew so many of Juliana's friends."

"I'm just good with names," I said with a smile.

"If he believed your other story then I guess he'll believe that one. Thank goodness you've saved yourself a little," Charlotte said.

"So what do you do now?" I asked.

He looked at the crowd of people. "Well, I'll assess everyone and their behavior while they're here of course. Plus, we've got the room bugged for recording."

My mouth dropped. "Can you do that?" Had he heard me talking to the ghosts? That would make him think I was crazy for sure.

"We have permission."

"I'm sure my parents would have gone along with that one hundred percent," Juliana said.

Another officer arrived.

"I'll be right back, okay?" Dylan said. "Don't hide under any plants again."

I smiled. "I'll be right here." I thought to keep that promise, but I spotted Hunter and Regina talking.

"Are you thinking what I'm thinking?" Charlotte said.

Juliana answered for me. "We have to go listen to them."

Since Dylan wasn't looking my way, I headed across the room to find out what those two were up to. They were still talking when I eased up behind them. Obviously, if they saw me they would recognize me and not say a word so I hid behind a tall woman until she gave me some strange looks. I had to think of some other way to get closer without Regina and Hunter seeing me. Unfortunately, there was no plant to hide behind. Taking my chances and hoping they didn't look over and notice me, I stepped a short distance away from the tall woman.

"Have you made any progress?" Regina asked.

Progress on what?

"No, but I'll let you know as soon as I find out anything."

That just wasn't cutting it. I had to find a better way to eavesdrop. Her cryptic messages weren't giving me what I needed. Was Dylan finding out more? I glanced to the left to see where he'd gone but couldn't find him. Was he looking for me behind the plant? Probably, since I'd told him I was staying put. He probably thought I never kept my word. I thought I was trustworthy and honest . . . until it came to solving a murder and then all of that went out the window.

Regina and Hunter were looking at me. I hurried away before they had a chance to say anything. I had probably made them mad. At the very least, they were suspicious.

"What did you find out?" Dylan asked.

I jumped and looked behind me. When I realized he was there, I said, "What do you mean?"

"Hunter and Regina. I saw you eavesdropping."

I guessed I had been obvious. "Well, Regina was asking if he had made any progress. I'm not sure what that was about."

The other officer called Dylan's attention again. He said he'd be right back and didn't even bother to tell me not to go anywhere.

Everyone was taking seats. The service was about to begin.

Somehow I had worked my way up to the front of the room. "Why is everyone looking at me?" I whispered out of the corner of my mouth.

"They probably think you're getting ready to speak, Cookie. You're standing by the ashes."

I stumbled backwards at the realization and lost my balance. Gasps rang out around the room. I quickly reached and grabbed the urn, catching it before it fell to the ground.

"Don't worry. Those things are sealed pretty tight so none of the ashes come out," Charlotte said.

"Good to know, Charlotte." I placed the urn back on the podium and hurried for the door. My face was completely red. I wondered if Dylan had seen that chaotic scene.

"You'll never be able to show your face around this funeral home again," Charlotte said from over my shoulder.

I ran out the door toward my car. I looked around for Dylan's car. I didn't see it, but luckily he wasn't out there waiting for me.

"Cookie, years from now you'll have to go to the next town over when it's time for your funeral. They probably will ban you from this place and others."

"I guess there are worse places to be banned from," I said. "Sorry I ruined your memorial service, Juliana." I just couldn't do anything right for her.

"It's okay, Cookie. Things happen."

I made it out of the parking lot and almost back to town before my cell rang. Dylan's number was on the screen. I guessed I might as well take the call and get it over with. "Hello?"

"You left in a hurry," he said.

I didn't want to admit what I'd done. "I figured I'd caused enough trouble and it was time for me to leave."

"Everything's fine. It's going lovely now. I just stepped out of the room."

"Sorry I didn't tell you sooner about my plans," I said.

"You actually got some valuable information and that's a good thing. I have to go, but I'll talk to you later, okay?"

"Sure. I'll talk to you later."

By the time I hung up I had reached It's Vintage Y'all. I was glad the funeral was behind me. Luckily, Dylan didn't seem upset about what had happened. Not sure if Regina was involved or not, I needed to figure out what I'd discovered.

Chapter 15

Cookie's Savvy Vintage Clothing
Shopping Tips

Find pieces that make
you comfortable and happy.

I flipped the sign to CLOSED, locked the door behind me, and headed down the sidewalk. It was the slow time of the day, so I was taking a break after lunch. I needed to make a quick trip to the post office. The weather was still a bit warm, but I felt a change in the air. With Charlotte and Juliana walking beside me we were like a paranormal version of Charlie's Angels. Especially since we were trying to solve a murder.

"You think Ken can find out anything useful from Regina?" Charlotte asked.

I didn't answer, wanting to keep the conversation about Regina to a minimum when Juliana was around.

"I think if she'll talk with anyone it would be Ken," Juliana said.

Charlotte and I looked at her.

"She'll definitely be charmed by him." Charlotte looked at me. "You need Dylan to tell you more about what the police know."

I stopped in front of the diner. "That's unlikely to happen. He's extremely professional."

"Why are we here?" Charlotte asked.

I opened the door. "I thought I'd get a slice of that delicious cherry pie."

"A moment on the lips, forever on the hips." Charlotte patted her hip.

Juliana chuckled.

"Thanks for the fitness advice, Charlotte. It was just what I wanted."

"She's so sarcastic," Charlotte whispered to Juliana.

Since we were about to step inside the diner with many people around, I couldn't answer. As I walked through the doorway, everyone was watching me. It always happened when anyone walked in. Just like in small towns everywhere, everyone wanted to know what was going on and what everyone else was doing.

Cutesy signs decorated the walls with sayings like KISS MY GRITS and WHAT'S COOKIN' GOOD LOOKIN'. Red-and-white checkered fabric covered the tables. Red leather booths lined the walls and tables and chairs were in the middle of the room.

Dixie Bryant was behind the counter. A petite brunette, she wore her usual uniform of white shirt, polka-dot apron, and jeans. She spotted me and waved me over. "Cookie! I'm glad you stopped by. I wanted to talk with you about buying an outfit for the fall festival."

"Dixie, you know you can stop by any time and I'll help you."

"What brings you by? Early dinner? Late lunch?" She picked up a menu. "We have new daily specials."

Charlotte tsk-tsked. "Pie is fattening."

I rolled my eyes.

Dixie looked to my left. "Is she still around?"

Charlotte huffed. "*She* has a name, Dixie. It's Charlotte. Just because you can't see me doesn't mean that I don't have a name."

"Actually, I just wanted to order a slice of cherry pie for later."

"No ice cream?" Dixie asked as she removed the pie from the glass display case.

"Ice cream! That's a lot of calories, Cookie. You'll have a little too much butter on the biscuit if you eat that." Charlotte patted her bottom.

Juliana laughed.

Apparently Charlotte was a comedian. She was just showing off for Juliana.

Dixie handed me the brown paper bag with the pie and looked around. "Is the murdered woman with you too?" she whispered.

I glanced around to see if anyone was listening. "She's right beside me."

Of course Dixie looked but couldn't see her. She

knew why Juliana was still there. "Do they have any leads?"

I shook my head. "I don't have much information."

Dixie motioned toward the entrance. "Well, here's your chance to find out."

Dylan was headed my way.

"Dixie's right. Ask him now," Charlotte said.

It wasn't that easy. By the look on his face, I didn't think he was there for a piece of pie.

"I'll talk to you soon, Dixie," I said as I headed over to him.

He hadn't taken his eyes off me since he'd entered the café.

"This looks serious," Charlotte said.

"Maybe he found my killer," Juliana said with hope in her voice.

That broke my heart.

"I've been looking everywhere for you," Dylan said. "You didn't answer your phone."

I pulled it from my pocket and saw that it was turned off. "Sorry. What's wrong?"

He peered around at the faces looking back at us. "Let's talk outside."

"This isn't good," Charlotte said.

I went with him outside the café. We stood on the sidewalk with Charlotte and Juliana beside me. Charlotte was tapping her foot against the pavement, apparently frustrated that Dylan hadn't told me what was wrong yet.

"I bet he has my killer," Juliana said.

I hoped he did for her sake. "What's wrong?" I asked again.

"I just found out that Victor has a criminal record. I'm concerned that this guy was in your shop and then your shop was broken into."

"This is bad, Cookie."

I looked over at Charlotte.

Dylan noticed my distraction. "Are you okay, Cookie? What are you looking at?"

I'd slipped. At least I hadn't spoken to her. It was only a matter of time until I slipped up and did that too. It was getting harder and harder to keep her presence from him. I hadn't told him because I just didn't think he would understand.

I waved off his question. "I just thought I saw someone."

He touched my arm. "If you're worried about this guy finding you, don't. As soon as I track him down, I'll tell him to leave town. Unless we can prove he was the one who broke into your shop, I can't arrest him."

"Interrogate him until he breaks," Charlotte said while pumping her fist in the air.

"Are you going back to your shop?" he asked me.

"Yes, I think it's best that I go back right now." I had planned on going to the post office, but the stamps could wait. I just wanted time to wrap my mind around what had happened. This Victor guy could be the killer. And he had been in my shop!

"I'll walk you back," Dylan said.

I clutched my bag of cherry pie as if it was my

lifeline. We crossed the street and stopped in front of my door.

"Do you think this man is the killer?" I asked.

"Good question, Cookie," Charlotte said.

Juliana stood next to Dylan, staring at him expectantly for his answer.

He stared at me for a moment. "We really don't have any evidence that would back that up."

"You don't have evidence, but do you think it? I mean, he has a criminal record and then he shows up in Sugar Creek right after the murder? Plus, he was asking about a hat." Okay, I sounded a little crazy, but I felt there was a connection.

"Good work, Cookie. You tell him," Charlotte said.

Dylan took my in his arms. "Cookie, I promise we'll solve this case. Please don't worry."

"He thinks you can't solve this crime. We'll show him, won't we, Cookie?" Charlotte placed her hands on her hips.

We will?

"I'll call you soon." Dylan kissed me good-bye and headed away from the shop.

"I like Dylan, really I do, but he needs to realize that you know a little something about this case," Charlotte said as we made our way into the shop.

It was still a bit spooky to think that the killer could have been inside. And that he still might be hanging around.

"I can't tell him that Juliana is here. And that I

have inside knowledge," I said as I turned on my computer.

Charlotte sat on the settee and drummed her fingers against the arm.

I sorted through a few pieces of clothing I'd recently purchased at an estate sale. I knew she was contemplating her next comment.

"Cookie, at some point you're probably going to have to tell Dylan about us."

I wasn't so sure about that. I figured that my ability to see ghosts would soon disappear just as it had so abruptly appeared in my life. I had no proof of that, but I was holding out hope.

Wind Song jumped down from her spot at the window. She leisurely strolled over to us and then jumped up onto the counter. Usually, that meant she wanted to be fed or wanted to give us a message with the tarot cards or Ouija board.

"Are you hungry, Wind Song?"

She meowed and pawed at my hand. I took that as a yes. Before I could get the food, she jumped from the counter and took off across the room. A scent of roses and a touch of musk floated through the air. Memories of my grandmother came rushing back.

"That was odd," I said.

"What's odd?" Charlotte asked.

"I just smelled my grandmother's favorite perfume . . . when Wind Song jumped down and ran across the room."

"Maybe it's your imagination," Charlotte said while studying her fingernails. She had a tendency to change her polish color often. Sometimes more than once a day.

Of course, when all she had to do was *think* of a color, it was pretty easy. One of the perks of being a ghost.

"My grandmother's favorite perfume was Wind Song. That's why I chose that name for the cat," I said to Juliana.

"That *is* a coincidence," Juliana said.

Wind Song stopped in front of the section of hats. She pawed at one of them and then turned back to look at me.

"I think she's trying to tell you something," Juliana said.

As I moved over to the hats, Wind Song strolled away. The hat she'd pointed out was a man's. I wasn't sure what message she was giving me. Something about that particular hat? "I guess she didn't have much to say."

"Maybe you can ask her to use the Ouija board," Charlotte said.

Wind Song was already asleep again in the sunshine. There was no need to ask. I'd learned early on that she did things when she was ready. She would tell me what she wanted me to know when she was ready. That kind of reminded me of my grandmother too. She'd only done something when she was ready.

I went back to work, trying to take my mind off Victor. I was curious though, if Juliana knew him. She'd been kind of secretive. After a few minutes of wondering, I asked her. "Juliana, do you know Victor?" I tagged a shirt and placed it on a hanger.

She shook her head. "I've never seen the man before. But right now I'm having a hard time remembering people I'd recently met."

"Why would he be interested in vintage clothing?" Charlotte asked.

I'd love to find that out. But how? I certainly didn't want to run into him again to ask. Finding out more about him was definitely in order.

Several customers came into the store so that kept me busy for the rest of the afternoon. I was grateful for the business and for the distraction.

I looked at the clock and turned off the computer. "I guess it's time to close for the day."

Charlotte jumped up from the settee. "Good. Now maybe we can get down to work."

"What do you mean? I'm planning on going home and taking a relaxing bath."

"That's not good use of your time, Cookie," Charlotte said.

"It's all I know to do right now. Maybe it will clear my mind so that I can come up with some brilliant plan."

I stepped out of the shop and locked the door. I was watching over my shoulder a lot more than usual lately.

Charlotte motioned with both hands as if waving in an airplane for landing. "It's scary out here, Cookie. You need to hurry up and get in the car."

Nights came sooner now and the streets of Sugar Creek were dark. Everyone had gone home for the day. Heather had left about an hour ago when she stopped by to say good night. I noticed a shadow not far away. A person was walking my way. I couldn't make out anything about the person, but based on the size, I assumed it was a man.

"This person is making me nervous, Cookie. You should get in your car now." Charlotte's voice raised a few decibels.

"Yes, hurry, Cookie," Juliana said.

The man quickened his steps. It did seem as if he was headed my way. I hurried toward my car but stumbled as I stepped down from the sidewalk.

"Cookie, are you okay?" Charlotte asked.

The man reached down and grabbed me. I didn't know how I would get out of the situation. I looked up and finally realized that it was Ken.

"Whew. Thank goodness it's him," Charlotte said.

I stumbled up from the pavement.

"Are you okay, Cookie?" he asked.

"Yes, I think I'm fine."

"You didn't even mess up your outfit," Charlotte said.

Leave it to her to point that out. That was the least of my worries. "I thought maybe you were the killer." I blew the hair out of my eyes.

He apologized. "I'm sorry I scared you. I was just walking back from the diner and thought I saw someone acting suspiciously around your store."

Chapter 16

Charlotte's Tips for a Fashionable Afterlife

❧

High heels never hurt your feet,
so go for the five-inch heels.

After thinking on it all night, I still had little idea what I should do to find Juliana's killer. I'd thought some rest and relaxation would ease my stress and I'd figure out what to do. That didn't happen. However, I thought wearing a cheery yellow dress would lift my mood.

Made of cotton, the 1960s dress had green, yellow, orange, and white ribbons that decorated the bodice and the waist. I paired it with my pale yellow 1970s open toe mules that had a crisscross strap around the heel. Carrying the little Prada bag I'd bought for a song certainly helped my mood too.

I met Heather at Glorious Grits for breakfast then made it to my shop. I opened the carrier door and Wind Song sashayed out and over to her spot in the sunshine. She certainly had her routine down. I went through my morning routine of paperwork and sorting through clothing.

When I pulled out a recently acquired wedding dress, Charlotte's eyes lit up.

"Don't get any ideas," I warned, hanging the dress on a rack. "People are always looking for vintage gowns."

Charlotte held her hands up. "It would look nice on you, that's all."

The wedding dress was absolutely stunning. I'd dated the dress to be from the late 1930s. The floor-length ivory silk gown had a bias cut with a wide pointed collar. It was sleeveless and partially open in the back with side snaps. A hook and eye closure was at the collar. I'd looked for any signs of damage and couldn't find a single hole, rip, or stain.

"Cookie, you seem upset today. What's wrong?" Charlotte asked.

I straightened the jewelry in the display case. "It's just that I'm worried about the break-in and not finding the killer."

Dylan hadn't called with word on Victor. I knew he'd call as soon as he heard anything, but the longer it went with no word, the more anxious I became.

"I told you we need to hunt this guy down. We'll find out the details on our own. Like I always said, if you want something done right you have to do it yourself."

"Sorry, Charlotte. I think that's a little too risky," I said.

Wind Song jumped down from the window and strolled past, not even looking at me.

I found myself watching her every move, wondering when she would provide the next message. It was crazy, waiting for a cat to talk to me. Somehow, I knew she was aware that I was watching her. It was like she could see me out of the corner of her eye. As she made her way to the hat display again, I exchanged a look with Charlotte and Juliana. I knew they were thinking the same thing as me and we moved closer to the hats.

Wind Song stretched out her paw and batted at one of the hats. It was a different one, but still a man's hat.

I stooped down to her level. "I don't know what your message is, Wind Song. You'll have to use the Ouija board to tell me what you're thinking."

The bell over the door chimed. I stood and turned my attention toward the man who had just entered the shop. He was tall with blond hair. Probably in his mid-twenties. He wasn't dressed in vintage, but then most people who came into my shop weren't.

The man noticed me and immediately put a smile on his face. "Good morning. Are you the owner?"

Maybe he's trying to sell something? "Yes, I'm the owner." I closed the distance between us.

Juliana stepped around me and made her way to stand beside him. She didn't take her eyes off him.

"My name is Hunter Owens." He extended his hand toward me.

I shook it and said, "Cookie Chanel. Welcome to It's Vintage Y'all. What can I help you with?"

Juliana was still transfixed on him. "Hunter was my boyfriend. Remember? He was talking with Regina at the funeral."

Yes, now I remembered where I'd seen him. Would he remember me from almost knocking over the urn?

"That explains the lovey-dovey look in her eyes," Charlotte said.

He seemed a little nervous. "Nice to meet you. I'd like to talk with you about Juliana McDaniel."

"I can't believe it's him. I can't believe he's standing here. I thought I'd never see him again after the funeral," Juliana said.

"Why is he here?" Charlotte asked.

Juliana didn't seem to hear or notice anything else in the room while Hunter was there.

Charlotte tossed her hands up. "Oh, good gravy. I can't get her to say anything, Cookie. Maybe you can."

Unfortunately, at the moment I couldn't ask Juliana what was going on, but my curiosity was piqued. Perhaps Hunter would tell me why he'd come by for a visit. "What would you like to talk about?"

"Juliana was my girlfriend. I know you were supposed to meet with her on *that* day."

"I'm sorry for your loss." Saying that felt weird since I was looking at Juliana when I said it.

"Thank you." He peered down at his white tennis shoes.

"And yes, I was supposed to meet her that day," I said.

"Juliana was writing a book about vintage, but you already know that." He stared at me.

"I'm sorry, Juliana, but your boyfriend is nuttier than a fruitcake," Charlotte said.

Juliana frowned. "Well, I think he has a reason to act strange. After all, he just lost me. He loved me."

"I don't doubt that he did. Nonetheless, he's acting strange."

I had to block out the chatter from the ghosts so that I could focus on Hunter.

"Anyway, the reason I came by was I wanted to know if perhaps she gave you any of her vintage items? I know she had some things she wanted you to take a look at. Did she give you anything before the tragedy?"

"Uh-huh. This is definitely strange," Charlotte said.

Apparently he was interested in getting the contents of Juliana's car too. Did he really think that I had the stuff? "I'm sorry, Mr. Owens. I didn't receive any of the items."

He stared at me for a moment. "Do you know what may have happened to the items she had?"

"I think the police probably have the contents of her car," I said.

"That's what I was afraid of." He gave some thought before asking, "Do you know how I could get them back?"

I shook my head. "No, I have no idea."

He ran his hand through his hair. "I really need them."

"Is there anything in particular that you're looking for?"

He paused.

While she stared at him, Charlotte said to me, "You need to find out more about this."

"There is nothing to find out. I think he's just looking out for me and wants to get my things back," Juliana said.

She was probably right . . . though Charlotte had put a doubt in my mind. Other people wanted the hat. Was he looking for it too? It seemed like I needed to get my hands on the hat. Obviously, it was important. I just couldn't understand why it was so important.

He never answered my question and continued frowning in silence.

Finally, I said, "I wish I could help you." Maybe it wasn't the hat that was important. Maybe it was something else they were looking for. Was there a connection between Hunter and Victor? What about the aunt? I had to find out more about all of them.

"I'll see you," Hunter said suddenly as he opened the door.

Needless to say, he left without a hat.

And I hoped I didn't see him again.

Chapter 17

Cookie's Savvy Vintage Clothing
Shopping Tips

*Some garments won't have a label. If you love the
item, don't let that stop you from buying it.*

Sometimes, Juliana had problems with remembering things. However, her memory apparently came back sometime after lunch. She called out, "Now I remember."

Charlotte jumped and clutched her chest. "What in the world is wrong with you? You scared me."

"Sorry, Charlotte. It's just that I remember where I got the items that were in my car. They'd belonged to Hunter's grandmother. She gave them to me." Juliana sighed, remembering. "She was a sweet lady."

"And what does that mean?" Charlotte said.

I stared at Juliana waiting for an answer. I had the same question.

"Maybe Hunter was asking for the items to give

them back to his grandmother." Juliana waved her hands through the air excitedly. "It makes sense, right?"

Charlotte tapped her fingers against the counter. "I suppose she does have a point."

I tapped my fingers against the counter too. "Yes, that's possible." I agreed. Knowing Juliana was happy that she'd finally remembered made me happy for her too.

"Do you remember why she gave the items to you?" I asked.

Juliana shrugged. "She just didn't want them anymore."

"Then I doubt she'd ask for them back," Charlotte said.

Wind Song weaved around my leg and meowed. She jumped on the counter. I gave her a treat and rubbed her head. She meowed in return.

Deep in thought, I said, "I need Hunter to tell me why he wanted that stuff."

"I remember his number. You could call him," Juliana said.

"What will I tell him when he asks how I got his number?"

Juliana tapped her index finger against her bottom lip. "That's a good question. I'm sure he would be suspicious. He's the suspicious type."

"I don't need that," I said.

"I know!" Juliana said enthusiastically. She'd had another eureka moment.

Charlotte rubbed her temples. "She has way too much energy."

Juliana didn't pay attention to what Charlotte said. "I remember where his grandmother lives. We could go visit her."

I rubbed Wind Song's head. "That's not a bad idea. She might be more willing to talk than your boyfriend. He seemed as if he wanted the items and nothing more. He'd want to know why I was so interested. Where does she live?"

"She's in Savannah," Juliana said. "I know exactly how to get there."

"Looks like we're taking a road trip," Charlotte said. "I hope she doesn't get us lost."

I hoped Juliana would be able to get the grandmother to talk with me. Maybe the woman wouldn't want to talk with a stranger. I also wanted to visit Fatima the psychic again. I looked out the window, realizing why it had been so slow all afternoon. Too nice outside. "I'll call Heather." I grabbed my phone.

"I wonder what Fatima would say if she knew that Heather really can't see ghosts."

"I don't suppose it's any of her business, Charlotte."

Charlotte shrugged. "I guess." By her tone I knew she wasn't convinced.

"Besides, she won't know anyway. I'm not going to tell her and thank goodness you can't."

"Maybe Fatima will be able to see me," Juliana said.

She had a point there.

I called Heather and told her to meet me as soon as possible. Five minutes later she was walking through the door.

"That was fast," I said.

"I really want to find out where Wind Song came from."

"Me too." I picked up my purse.

I thought about taking Wind Song along, but she probably wouldn't enjoy the ride much. I said good-bye and told her that we would be back soon to pick her up. She seemed content to stare out the window.

I turned the sign to CLOSED, locked the door of the shop behind me, and we all raced to the car with Heather claiming the front seat. Of course, Charlotte wasn't happy about that. She always thought she should be shotgun. Heather threatened to sit on top of her, so it was a whole big argument . . . all relayed through me. Finally, Charlotte gave up and got in the back with Juliana.

"I'll have you know I get car sick in the backseat," Charlotte said.

"That's not possible anymore, Charlotte." I looked at her in the rearview mirror.

We made the beautiful drive to Savannah and through the historic section of town. Spanish moss covered trees draped across the roads.

"Your driving scares me to death," Charlotte said.

"That's not possible either," I said.

Juliana had been right. She knew exactly where his grandmother lived. We drove by the house, but then decided to go by the psychic's place first. We pulled up to the psychic shop. Heather had called to make sure Fatima was there, but she was only going to be there for a short time so we needed to hurry.

I found a spot to park and thank goodness it wasn't parallel parking. We hopped out.

"I can't wait to hear what she has to say," Heather said.

We stepped into the shop and Charlotte said, "It stinks in here."

"It doesn't smell bad, Charlotte. It just smells like sandalwood and whatever."

"It's just so strong."

"You can't even smell. You're dead."

She quirked an eyebrow. "Well, you don't have to remind me."

Luckily, no one was in the shop and looking at me strangely for talking to nothing, but being that it was a psychic shop maybe they wouldn't have been surprised. Heather and I walked around a little bit, waiting for Fatima to finish her phone call.

Finally, she stepped over to us. "That was a fast trip from Sugar Creek."

"Oh no, we were almost here when I called. I suppose it would've made more sense if we had called before we left Sugar Creek, but we were a little anxious," Heather said.

"You have questions for me?" She looked from Heather to me.

"She has questions." Heather pointed to me.

It felt a little strange trying to figure out why a cat was psychic. "Heather told you over the phone about the white cat that mysteriously showed up at my shop. Well . . ." I hesitated.

The woman said, "Yes? And the cat uses the tarot cards and the Ouija board."

It sounded even stranger when someone else said it.

I felt a little uneasy at her directness. "Yes, that's right."

"Did you bring the cat with you?" she asked, looking all around.

"No, she stayed home. She's a little finicky on long rides." I'd taken her to my parents' house once and that hadn't ended well. She kept getting into my mother's health food and my mother had to throw it away. "You saw the cat here?" I asked.

"Yes, it was probably right before she showed up at your place. How she got from here to Sugar Creek, I don't know."

"How can you be sure it was the same cat? I mean, there are a lot of white cats around."

"She was only here for a day, but it was odd when she was here. She kept trying to get to the tarot cards."

That was too big a coincidence. "You don't know how the cat got into the store?" I asked.

"The first time I ever saw her she was present at a séance."

"The cat was part of the séance?" Charlotte asked.

Fatima looked in the direction of Charlotte, but she didn't answer. I wondered if she could see her too. After all, she was a psychic. She wasn't just pretending like Heather. Or was she?

"I don't know where the cat came from. One minute she wasn't here and the next she was sitting by my feet."

"That's exactly how she showed up at my place," I said.

Wind Song was a beautiful cat so I was sure Fatima had enjoyed having her. She'd said the cat had taken off before she'd gotten too close.

"Actually, she's changed my life," I said with a smile.

"Sometimes we get just we need when we're least expecting it," Fatima said.

"So who was having the séance?" I asked.

"I can't give specific information."

"Of course not," I said but had hoped she would.

"A woman from Tybee Island had been trying to make contact with loved ones."

"You don't remember a name?"

"Cookie, she just told you she couldn't give that information," Charlotte said.

Well, it didn't hurt to ask.

Fatima shook her head. "I don't remember who the woman was."

"Maybe the cat belonged to that woman," Juliana said.

It was possible, but I would never be able to find out. My parents lived in Tybee Island, but that would be of little help in figuring out this mystery.

"If you happen to find out any other information, would you contact me?" I asked.

She agreed. "Yes, you own the vintage shop in Sugar Creek."

I knew my outfit gave it away. "Yes, that's me."

"I'll certainly be in touch if I think of anything."

"Thank you," I said.

"Well, this was a wasted trip," Charlotte said.

Fatima looked over in her direction again. I wanted to ask if she could see the ghosts, but her phone rang.

"I have to get that. Have a safe drive back to Sugar Creek." She took off for the phone.

Heather and I walked out of the shop. Charlotte and Juliana weren't behind me.

"Where are they?" I asked.

Heather shrugged. Of course she couldn't see them. I peeked in the window and saw that they were still in the shop.

Fatima looked up as I hurried back through the door.

I waved my hand. "I forgot something," I said, stepping in front of Charlotte and Juliana and giving them the glare.

They finally marched out of the store with me.

Chapter 18

Charlotte's Tips for a Fashionable Afterlife

*Shop 'til you drop
has a whole new meaning now.*

"I may never find out how Wind Song knows to communicate with the cards and Ouija board," I said as we walked toward my car.

"I won't have you being negative. You have to remain positive," Charlotte said with a wave of her hand.

"I'm positive, but I'm also realistic." I opened the car door and slid in.

Heather climbed in on the other side. "I assume Charlotte wants you to stay positive. I think she's right."

"Thank you, Heather." Charlotte sat a little straighter.

Wow, they had agreed again. It was happening more and more. At least they weren't arguing.

I started the car and pulled out. "I'll try to be more positive."

"Positive thinking attracts positive things," Charlotte said. "You should do meditation."

"Seriously, Charlotte? You are one of the highest strung people I've ever met. I've heard the stories about you."

"You shouldn't believe everything you hear. There's a ton of gossip in Sugar Creek." Charlotte applied lipstick while holding a compact.

Where had she gotten that? She had ghostly makeup? Anyway, I hated to break it to her, but it wasn't gossip.

After a short drive, we pulled up in front of Hunter's grandmother's house.

"What's her name?" I asked.

"Violet Owens," Juliana said.

"What will I say to her?" I asked.

We stared at the house. I wasn't going up to the door without a plan.

"That's a good question." Juliana tapped her index finger against her bottom lip.

"We have to come up with something," Charlotte said.

Juliana held up her finger. "I know! Just tell her you're a friend of Hunter's. She will do anything for him. Any friend of Hunter's is a friend of hers."

"Won't she be suspicious of that? What if she tells him?" I asked.

"You're overthinking this," Charlotte said.

I had a tendency to do that a lot, but I didn't think that was the case at the moment.

"I'll go with you," Heather offered as she opened the car door.

Still reluctant, I opened the car door. "Okay, let's do this."

Heather and I walked to the door.

"Here goes nothing." I rang the doorbell.

"Everything will be fine." Heather patted my arm.

I stood a little straighter. "Do I look okay?"

"You look fabulous as always," Heather said.

"I still say you should have worn the red heels," Charlotte said.

As if I would listen to anything she said. Suddenly the door opened and the woman stared at me without speaking. She was petite with her hair up in a bun. Sprinkles of gray ran through the dark strands. She wore blue pants and a pink blouse.

The visit could become awkward quickly. Apparently I needed to speak before she slammed the door in my face. I thought Juliana had said she was *nice*.

"Ms. Owens, my name is Cookie Chanel."

Charlotte leaned on the front of the house. "I don't think she's impressed."

Violet continued to stare at me.

I shrugged a little. "Anyway, I'm friends with your grandson Hunter."

Her eyes widened and she opened the door. "Why didn't you say so earlier? Come on in here." She grabbed my arm and pulled me into the house. Next, she took Heather by the arm and escorted her inside. "Come in here and sit down."

She guided us to the living room. It was a small space with not a lot of furniture or knickknacks.

However, a table was full of pictures of Hunter. Violet offered us iced tea and then immediately started talking about him. Apparently, he'd placed second in the spelling bee in second grade and won the track meet his junior year of high school.

I had to move the conversation along. "Does Hunter stop by to see you often?"

"Not nearly often enough. I realize he has a busy life." To emphasize her point, Violet gave a little sigh.

"Mention me," Juliana said.

"It's tragic what happened to his girlfriend." I quirked an eyebrow, wondering if Violet would answer.

"Yes, it is, but he had nothing to do with it." She shifted in the chair.

"Wow. That was an odd thing to say. No one is accusing him of murder . . . yet." Charlotte arched a brow.

"And they won't be either," Juliana said.

"Do you have any idea who did it?" I asked Violet.

"She was a sweet girl, so I can't imagine anyone would want her dead." Violet drummed her fingernails against the chair.

"When is the last time you saw Hunter?" I asked.

"Good question," Charlotte said.

"It's been awhile. Actually, I think it was right after Juliana was murdered. I've talked with him on the phone. He came by looking for some stuff he had in one of my bedrooms but couldn't find it. I was really upset because I feel as if I lost it."

"Do you know what he lost?" I asked.

"No, he didn't tell me. I think that's why he hasn't been back around." Violet fidgeted again.

"The poor thing," Charlotte said. "He needs to get over here and visit his grandmother."

"I'm sure that's not the reason. Like you said, he's just busy." I attempted to comfort her, but what could I do?

"If I show you the room, would you be able to offer a fresh set of eyes?" Violet looked out the window.

Was she expecting someone? I exchanged a look with Heather.

"Tell her yes. You want a chance to snoop around that room. I can't believe how trusting this woman is," Charlotte said. "I mean you two are complete strangers."

Juliana shook her head. "Like I said, using Hunter's name is like the secret passcode for entry."

Heather gave a subtle nod in agreement, so I said, "Sure we'd be happy to help you."

We followed her down the hallway to the bedroom on the right. The walls were painted a pale yellow with beige carpet on the floor. It was empty except for a large armoire between the two windows on the far end of the room.

"This is where the vintage items had been stored. She brought me in here to look at them before she gave them to me. They'd been stored in the armoire." Juliana hurried over to the massive mahogany cabinet against the wall.

Had Hunter hidden something in the same spot where those vintage items were kept? Was there a link? "This is a lovely piece." I couldn't resist and opened the armoire. *Empty*.

Violet looked around. "Perhaps he'd put something

in the purse I gave to Juliana. As you can see, it would be kind of hard to misplace something in this room. There's not a lot here. I just don't know what it might have been."

Juliana shook her head. "If it was something other than the hat, why would Victor be looking for the hat?"

"Well, now you need access to the items the police have," Charlotte said to me.

Yeah, like that would be possible. The room was so empty it almost looked as if Violet was moving out.

"Are you planning on selling the house?" I asked.

"Hunter says that maybe we could sell the house." Violet peeked out the window again.

I hated to tell her, but it sounded like that wouldn't be the best idea. I doubted she wanted to hear it from me. Anything Hunter said was what she wanted to hear. I moved across the room and looked out the window. I had a view of the neighbor's brick house. It was almost identical to Violet's place. Then again, most of the houses on the street looked the same. A for sale sign stood in the front yard of the house next door.

"I'm sure the houses sell quickly around here. Looks like you would have some competition though." I gestured toward the house next door.

Juliana moved beside me. Charlotte stood by the door, looking as if she was bored and wanted to leave.

"Hunter was talking with the man who lives next door. He was the one who suggested that we sell the house." Violet crossed her arms in front of her chest.

"Is he a realtor?" I asked.

She shook her head. "Not that I know of. His name is Victor."

I froze. "Victor?"

Charlotte scooted over and stood beside me. That had gotten her attention. I was just about ready to ask if she knew his last name when I spotted him in his front yard. I couldn't believe he lived next door to Violet. I gestured to Juliana and Charlotte.

"I can't believe it," Charlotte said. "We have to find out more about him."

Victor disappeared into his house.

"So your grandson talked to the man next door?" I asked.

Violet nodded. "Yes, they had developed a bit of a friendship lately. He seems like a nice enough man. I've met him a few times."

"Hunter never mentioned anything about being friends with the neighbor." Juliana stared at the house next door.

"If they were up to no good, he probably wouldn't have told you." Charlotte cast a sympathetic look at Juliana.

Juliana frowned. "I know I can trust Hunter. Are you suggesting that he had something to do with my murder?"

When Violet wasn't looking, I motioned for Charlotte to apologize.

"I'm sorry," she said less than enthusiastically.

"Apology accepted." Juliana sounded sincere . . . as if she truly meant it.

"You should go over there and find out what he is up to," Charlotte said to me.

She was forgetting one little important thing. Dylan had said Victor was dangerous. I had to tell Dylan where to find this guy.

"Does he live there alone?" I asked.

"As far as I know," Violet said.

"So you only have to worry about one person when you go over there," Charlotte said.

Yeah, one guy who was wanted by the police.

"Thanks for inviting us in, Violet. I'm sorry we couldn't help you find what Hunter was looking for. I'm sure he isn't mad at you though."

"I hope so," she said around a sigh.

I gave her a big smile. "I know so."

Violet patted my arm. "Will you come back sometime?"

She was so sweet how could I say no?

She added a clincher. "Maybe I'll have some vintage items for you. I will have to look in the attic. They belonged to my grandmother."

My eyes widened. I wished I had time to look up there. Just the mention of vintage made my heart go pitty-pat.

Violet walked us to the door. "I'll call you if I find the clothing."

"Thanks!"

We waved as we walked down the path toward the car. She watched us from the doorway for a while and then finally shut the door. The look in her eyes when we left gave me a strange vibe, but I couldn't quite put my finger on it.

"There has to be a connection between the items

Hunter was looking for and the items Juliana had in her car," I said.

"So are you going over there to talk with Victor?" Charlotte asked.

"No way." I inched closer to my car. "He is too dangerous."

"You know you want to," Charlotte teased.

I hated when she was right. "Okay, but we're only going a little closer. It's not like I'm going to ring the doorbell."

"Maybe he'll invite you in for iced tea."

I tiptoed across the lawn.

"It's not like you're trying to sneak up on a wild animal, Cookie."

"Just be careful, Cookie. This makes me nervous," Juliana said.

"Me too," I said. "I just can't go peek in his windows."

Charlotte was always so impatient. "Okay, if you're going to be a baby about it, we should just leave."

"Good idea." I spun around and headed back toward the car.

"Who's that?" Charlotte pointed backwards.

I looked over my shoulder. A woman had stepped out of Victor's home. Between the giant hat she wore and the trees in the front yard blocking the view, I couldn't see her well enough to identify her. "Maybe it's his wife or sister?"

Heather and I hurried over to my car and jumped in.

"Wait. Here comes Victor. You should follow them, Cookie," Charlotte said.

"I'm not sure that's a good idea," Juliana said.

"You don't think anything is a good idea. How will we solve this case if we don't do anything?" Charlotte said.

"You think everything is a good idea. I don't want Cookie to end up like me. Do you?" Juliana glared at Charlotte.

For once, Charlotte was speechless. It may have been the first time I'd ever seen her that way.

I didn't want to see them argue and started the car as Victor got into his car with the woman and they took off. "Okay, maybe we will follow them just a little bit."

Charlotte smirked. "See, Cookie loves this just as much as I do."

Heather buckled her seatbelt. "Let's do this."

Juliana remained quiet in the backseat. We followed them down the street and then turned onto the main street. Unfortunately, we hit a bit of traffic.

"We don't know where they are going," Heather said. "It will be hard to keep up."

"Write down their license plate number in case we lose them." I pointed at the car up ahead.

Heather pulled a receipt from her bag and wrote the number down on the back. It was a good thing. Just as she finished, Victor made a sudden right turn. I couldn't get over to do the same.

"You lost them," Charlotte said.

"It was as if they knew you were following them," Heather said.

I released a deep breath. "I think they knew."

"It's probably for the best anyway," Juliana said.

I made the next turn and headed for the highway.

It was getting dark. "We'll just head back to Sugar Creek. I'll give Dylan the license plate number and maybe he can find out more information."

"You'll have to tell him why you were following this criminal," Heather said.

I tapped the steering wheel in aggravation. "Good point."

Once again, I may never find out the answers to all my questions.

Chapter 19

Cookie's Savvy Tips for Vintage Shopping

❧

Sometimes the best part of vintage shopping is the thrill of the hunt.

I tapped my fingers against the steering wheel in rhythm to Buddy Holly singing "Peggy Sue" as I mulled over all we'd learned. "You know what? I think Hunter hid something in the hat and that's why he and Victor seem so anxious to find it. Now what should I do?"

Everyone stared at me but didn't respond.

"I should just ask Hunter what he hid." I looked in the rearview mirror at Juliana. "Do you think he would tell me?"

She shrugged. "I don't know anything anymore. Everything I thought has turned out to be different."

"He's staying at a hotel in town, right?" Heather asked.

"That's what Dylan said." I steered the car.

"You're going there now?" Charlotte asked, but based on the tone of her voice it was more like an order.

"Yes, I'll go now."

Charlotte settled into the seat. "I knew you'd do the right thing."

When we reached Sugar Creek, I turned onto Highway 10 and headed toward the Red Rose Hotel.

"Are you just going to come out with the question or will you ease into it?" Heather asked.

I made the next right and pulled into the hotel parking lot. "I guess I should ease into it. That way it won't seem so confrontational."

"That's good," Juliana said. "He doesn't like confrontation."

"Juliana says he doesn't like confrontation," I repeated for Heather.

"Who does?" Heather said.

Everyone looked at Charlotte.

"I'm not afraid to tell anyone that either." Charlotte punctuated the sentence with a point of her index finger.

I laughed. "Point proven."

Eying a parking spot toward the front, I headed that way. Within a second, a bang rang out and the front window was pierced. Everyone in the car screamed. I punched the gas and took off, narrowly avoiding the other parked cars. My heart raced and my body shook. Needless to say, it was difficult to drive, but I managed to get away from the hotel.

"What was that?" Charlotte yelled.

Heather inched up in the seat. "Look! There's a

bullet hole in the windshield. Someone shot at your car!"

Fear raced through my body. Was it an accident? Or had someone shot at me on purpose?

"You're lucky to be alive, Cookie," Charlotte said.

"Are you okay, Heather?" I touched her arm.

She stared straight ahead and seemed to be in shock. I'd never seen her speechless.

"We were almost killed," I said breathlessly. "A bullet went right through the windshield."

"Are you sure it was a bullet?" Juliana asked.

"Considering there's a bullet in the backseat, I'm pretty sure that's what it was," Charlotte said.

I pulled in behind a building down the street, stopped the car, and took a deep breath. Leaning over the seat, I spotted the bullet. I reached back, picked it out of the cushion, and put it in my pocket.

"This is scary," Juliana said. "It's like when someone shot at my car. We all know how that ended."

Luckily, no one was hurt. The windshield hadn't even shattered.

"Do you think it was aimed at me?" I asked.

"Even if it wasn't you need to call the police. People can't just shoot guns in a parking lot." Heather had finally snapped back to attention. "How dare they do that! You have to call Dylan so he can arrest them and throw them in jail."

I knew by the tone of her voice that she was angry.

"Heather's right," Charlotte said.

With a shaky hand, I dialed Dylan. Now I had to really explain why we were there.

He answered on the first ring. "Detective Valentine."

"Dylan, I've been shot at." I rushed the words.

"Cookie, where are you?" he asked with alarm.

Okay, that wasn't the best way to start the call. I'd caused him to panic.

"We're okay though," I added. That was little help now that I'd already scared him. "My car window is broken." No one messes with my Buick! I took another deep breath and told him what had happened and where we were.

"I'll be there soon." He hung up.

What would we do until the police arrived? Even though I thought we were hidden behind the building, I was afraid the shooter would find us. My car was kind of a showstopper. Everyone noticed it. What if they shot at us again and were successful? The thoughts sent a shiver down my spine.

It couldn't have been more than a minute until the cop cars pulled up. Dylan whizzed the cruiser into the lot, screeched to a stop beside me, and jumped out. As soon as I climbed out of my car, he wrapped his arms around me and his earthy scent encircled my body.

"Wow, that's some police service," Charlotte said.

"Are you okay?" He looked me in the eyes.

I pulled away a bit and used my hand to mimic a gun. "The bullet went through the windshield."

"We've blocked off the parking lot of the hotel. We'll have to check your car and test anything we find."

"Thank you for coming here." Emotion overwhelmed me. Blinking back tears, I hoped I didn't break down completely.

"Cookie, you know I'd do anything for you." He touched my cheek. "We're searching for the shooter and interviewing witnesses."

"I just hope they find something." The hole in my windshield sent shivers down my spine.

"Why were you there?" Dylan asked.

"Make up an excuse," Charlotte said.

Usually I wouldn't agree with her, but I figured I would leave out a teensy bit of the truth. Lying to Dylan made me unhappy, but it was necessary. Telling him that Juliana had wanted to see Hunter wasn't an option. I could only imagine *that* conversation. It would go something like "Well Dylan, Juliana's ghost wanted to see her boyfriend."

Dylan wouldn't believe anything I said for the rest of my life. He knew that Hunter was staying at the hotel. And he knew that I knew. Oh, I might as well tell the truth. Dylan would see right through my lie. My internal debate was out of hand.

I quickly flipped back to thinking that my little fib was a good idea and said, "Okay, to be honest, I just wanted to see if Hunter was still in town." I attempted to keep my expression neutral so he wouldn't be able to see my lie. Besides, it wasn't a lie totally. I just hadn't told him the *full* truth.

Dylan ran his hand through his thick dark hair. "Cookie, this has gotten way too serious. You can't continue getting yourself into these situations."

"What does he think he can do to change that?" Charlotte paced beside the Buick.

"He can solve my murder," Juliana said.

"Cookie, I have to be honest with you. I'm afraid for your safety." A frown darkened his brow.

"I understand, but I had no way of knowing I would be shot at just by driving through the parking lot. It may have nothing to do with Juliana's murder."

"He can't argue with that," Charlotte said.

Dylan was about to respond when another officer walked up and pulled him to the side.

"I'll be right back, Cookie." He walked a bit farther away with the officer.

"What do you think's going on?" Heather asked.

"Maybe they caught the shooter," I said.

"I'll go find out," Charlotte had taken two steps when Dylan headed toward us. "Never mind." She waved her hand. "They found Juliana's aunt nearby."

"What does that mean?" Juliana asked.

"Aha!" Charlotte said. "So she is the killer."

When Dylan arrived, I asked, "Did Regina confess?"

The expression on his face changed immediately, becoming shadowed with suspicion. "Regina stated that she doesn't have a gun and she would never hurt Cookie. We found no gun on her person."

"What made the police ask her in the first place?" Juliana asked.

"She was near Hunter's car. That's why we asked her in the first place." Dylan answered Juliana's question without realizing it. "Apparently Victor had asked her to meet him there."

"What did he want with her?" I asked.

Dylan motioned to another officer and then

focused his attention on me again. "She said she didn't know."

"Then why would she meet him?" Charlotte asked.

"We're looking for Victor now."

I supposed it was time to tell him that I knew where Victor lived. I looked down at my feet. "Yeah about that. I know where he lives." I felt Dylan's stare.

"And how do you know that?"

I looked up and shrugged. "I just happened to pass by and saw him?"

Dylan shook his head.

"Okay, I was visiting Hunter's grandmother. She said Victor lives next door. I saw him there."

"Why would you do that?" Dylan asked.

"I just thought maybe she could offer information." I stared at my shoes.

"We've already talked with her."

I looked up again. "Yes, well maybe she forgot something." I tucked a loose strand of hair behind my ear.

"I know you're trying to help, Cookie, but we have everything under control. Do you not trust me?"

"No, it's not that," I said.

He didn't take his eyes off me. "I'm not so sure."

"Now you've hurt his feelings, Cookie. Apologize right now," Charlotte said.

I shook my head at her. "So if you know where Victor lives, why don't you go get him?"

"We don't know that he did anything wrong. Besides he doesn't live there."

"But I saw him there. He was with a woman. They

left together. He even tried to convince Hunter's grandmother to sell her house." I rushed my words.

"It sounds like you spent quite a bit of time there." Dylan quirked an eyebrow. When I didn't answer, he continued. "It's Victor's aunt's house. She's out of the country right now and he's house-sitting."

"Oh, I guess she led me to believe that he lives there now," I said.

"Nonetheless, we're keeping an eye on him." Dylan crossed his arms in front of his chest. "It's not as if I wouldn't have found out what you're up to. I'm sure it will get back to me soon enough that you were there."

"If you are watching Victor, why don't you have anyone watching Hunter?" I asked.

"Yeah, tell him, Cookie," Charlotte said.

"Well, that's a problem we're addressing."

"If a police officer had been at the hotel, maybe we wouldn't have been shot at." I looked over at my car. "Is it okay if I leave now? It's been a long day."

"Yes, you can go. Cookie, I'm sorry if I sounded rough, but I just don't want you hurt."

"He also doesn't want you involved with the investigation," Juliana said.

As usual, Charlotte had something to add. "It's because he thinks Cookie is questioning his skills as a detective."

All this ghost chatter was giving me a headache.

Chapter 20

Charlotte's Tips for a Fashionable Afterlife

You never have to worry about
being out of style.

Thank goodness the garage was right around the corner from my shop. Leaving my car there the next morning to have the windshield repaired was a tough thing to do, but I was assured they'd take good care of her and have it ready by end of the day.

Back in my shop, I tried to relax from the stress of the day before. I was still worried about Heather. She hadn't dealt well with our brush with death. It was understandable. I just felt terrible that I had put her in that situation.

She'd said she'd known the consequences and that it had been her decision to go along to the hotel, but I still felt bad. I'd have to make it up to her.

I worked in the windows of my shop, setting up the displays. Styling the windows always brought me comfort and relaxation. Although at the moment it seemed almost impossible to do that, I was styling the windows with a jack-o-lantern and skeletons for Halloween. It was the busiest time of year for me. Everyone liked to shop for costumes. Since I knew vintage items weren't just for Halloween, I'd dressed one of the mannequins in a fifties poodle skirt.

A noise caught my attention and I looked over my shoulder. Wind Song was sitting on the counter. If I hadn't known better I would have sworn she motioned for me to come over with her paw. I set down the blouse in my hand and walked over to her.

"Is everything okay?" Charlotte asked from the settee where she and Juliana were lounging.

Wind Song meowed loudly.

"Is she hungry?" Juliana asked. "Maybe she's sick?"

"No, I can tell by her meow that she wants to use the Ouija board."

I dialed Heather. "It's time. Bring the Ouija board."

Within seconds, she walked through the door.

I said, "She wants to give us a message."

Heather placed the board on the counter and Wind Song immediately placed her paw on the planchette. We watched as she spelled out a word. *D. I. S . . .*

"Disappeared?" Heather rubbed her arms. "That sends a shiver down my spine."

"What does she mean?" Charlotte asked.

"I don't know, but it's a little scary."

"It has to be some kind of warning," Heather said.

That's what I was worried about. My phone rang and we all jumped. We were a little on edge.

I peered at the screen. "It's Dylan."

"Cookie, how are you?" Concern filled his voice.

"I'm okay now. My car is in the shop and I'm working on the window displays." I left out the part about talking to my psychic cat, of course.

"It amazes me how well you bounce back from this stuff," he said.

"I have to be strong. There's no time to let the stress get me down."

I sensed from the tone of his voice that concern wasn't the only reason for his call. I waited for him to drop the bad news on me.

"I have something to tell you," he finally said.

"What happened?" I asked.

"Victor and Hunter have disappeared."

"What? They left together?"

"What is it?" Charlotte, Juliana, and Heather all asked the same question at the same time.

"We don't know if they are together. Hunter has checked out of the hotel and we've lost track of Victor."

"If they both disappeared at the same time that must mean they're together."

"Disappeared?" Charlotte echoed.

It hit me. Had Wind Song been trying to tell me about Hunter and Victor? Had the cat known it even before Dylan had called?

"So it they aren't around at least it's a little safer?" I asked.

"That's if they were involved."

I glanced over at Juliana. I knew she didn't like to

think that Hunter could have had something to do with her murder.

"It still might not be safe. Just don't let your guard down." The edge to Dylan's voice warned of the seriousness of the situation.

"I never let my guard down. Even if there wasn't a murderer running around, I pay attention."

"We'll still be on the lookout for them. As of right now, we don't have anything to link them to the crime. Just being suspicious isn't enough."

"I'll make sure to be on the lookout," I said.

He changed the subject. "Are you free for dinner?"

I glanced over at Charlotte and Juliana, feeling as if I had to ask them if I was free. What was I thinking? "Sure, I can make it."

"I was hoping you'd say that," Dylan said.

Would he be upset if I asked him about the case at dinner? Probably so. I would try to keep the topic out of the conversation unless he mentioned it. But would it be wrong if I steered the conversation that way and made him think it was his idea? Yeah, he probably wouldn't fall for that either.

"I'll see you tonight," he said.

"See you then," I said and clicked off the call.

"What was that all about?" Charlotte asked right away.

Wind Song jumped down and pranced over to the window.

"The police can't find Victor or Hunter."

Juliana walked away. That was a little too much for her to handle.

"Uh-huh. Just as I suspected." Charlotte tapped her fingers against the counter.

"What's that?" I asked.

She paused. "I don't know for sure, but I can guarantee that it isn't good. You're meeting Dylan tonight?"

I straightened a blue and white Dior polka-dot dress on the hanger. "He asked, so I figured why not."

"Maybe he'll have more information for you."

"I don't want to bring it up. He already doesn't want me to be involved."

Charlotte crossed her arms in front of her waist. "Getting what you want isn't always possible."

Didn't I know that. I went back to dressing the window.

Juliana and Charlotte were chatting away. My dinner with Dylan had sparked their excitement. Not only were they excited about the potential clues they thought we'd discover, but Charlotte was already planning my outfit for the evening. I pretended I couldn't hear them.

"Cookie doesn't look good in orange. Why she continues to wear that color is beyond me."

"Orange is a good color for fall," I said.

"I knew you were listening." Charlotte laughed.

That was a dirty trick.

Chapter 21

Cookie's Savvy Tips for Vintage Shopping

*Add a vintage hat to your outfit
for a fun pop of pizazz.*

I'd retrieved my car from the garage before dinner with Dylan and was driving from Sugar Creek to Tybee Island early the next morning. The boutique was closed on Sundays and my parents Hank and Margaret had scheduled a cookout. It was a scenic drive. Glancing in the rearview mirror at Juliana and at Charlotte next to me, I grinned. My parents had no idea I had extra guests coming along . . . those who wouldn't require food.

Speaking of food, I knew my mother would have everything but real meat. Preferring health food that tasted like tree bark, she was a fan of tofu and seeds. It was one of her enduring qualities. My father would sneak in hamburgers and hot dogs for some of us.

We pulled up to the house and I shut off the car.

Being right near the water, the little blue house with white shutters looked very coastal. Pretty flowers were everywhere. I got out of the car and headed up to the door.

Before I reached the porch my mother swung open the door, raced out and wrapped her arms around me, embracing me with a hug. The scent of Patchouli swirled around her. Like most days, she wore a long linen skirt that reached down to her knees, and a silk purple and yellow blouse. Luckily, she didn't have socks on with her Birkenstock sandals.

We were a couple opposites. I wore a pair of 1950s black cigarette pants, a red and white polka-dot silk blouse with a tapered waist, and red patent leather flats. My vintage Louis Vuitton Speedy completed my outfit perfectly.

Juliana eyed my mother up and down. "You look nothing like your mother."

"She doesn't get her fashion sense from her mother." Charlotte shivered. "I don't see how her mother wears that itchy fabric."

Juliana agreed. "Me either."

My father popped out from the back porch when he heard our voices. He held a spatula in one hand and wore an apron that read KISS THE COOK. A giant chef hat rested lopsided on his head. "There's my girl. Come over here and give me a hug."

I hurried over. My dad wrapped his strong arms around me and hugged me. He smelled like fresh salt air and hamburgers as I hugged him back.

"Are you ready for a burger?" He waved the spatula as if it were a wand.

My mother gave a disapproving frown.

I winked at my dad. That was our usual signal that I wanted my burger well done and with cheese.

"Be careful with that spatula. She doesn't want to smell like beef. Your father gets that smell everywhere." My mother took me by the arm and pointed toward the kitchen. "Come help me with some goodies."

Dad just shook his head and went back to the grill.

I doubted that they were goodies. More like tree bark and bird food. We walked into the kitchen and childhood memories immediately flooded my mind. Even though it was a different house than I'd grown up in, the kitchen was decorated the same. Blue-and-white checkered curtains hung on the window over the sink. My mother's vast collection of coffee mugs took up every available space. No matter where my parents moved, it always felt like home. The smell of spices and herbs lingered in the air.

I started pulling out the plastic plates that we used for the patio.

"Isn't Dylan coming today? He is such a nice young man." My mother pulled out kale from the refrigerator.

I couldn't believe my mother said that. She'd never liked anyone I'd dated.

"He's going to try." I reached for the plastic cups. "He had a few things to wrap up first."

"Well, I hope he can make it," my mother said, pulling out bowls from the shelf. "Can you get something out of that cabinet for me?"

"Sure," I said.

I hoped I remembered which one. The drawers

had been rearranged since they'd moved into the new house. With the first drawer I tried, I quickly discovered that wasn't where the utensils were stored. The drawer was full of papers, pens, and other miscellaneous items.

Essentially it was a junk drawer, but there was something that stuck out to me right away. The word *Fatima* was written on a card. I pulled the card from the drawer. What an odd discovery. My mother had never believed in paranormal stuff, which was kind of odd. Of all people I knew, I would have expected her to be spiritually inclined.

"Why do you have this card?" I asked, holding the card up.

My mother's eyes widened. She had a funny expression, as if she'd been caught eating the birthday cake before a party.

She took the card from my hand and chuckled. "A few girlfriends and I were in town shopping and they insisted that we go in. It was just a silly little thing. I should have thrown the card away." She stuffed the card into the pocket of her skirt.

I had more questions for her, but when the doorbell rang, I knew that I'd temporarily lost my chance.

"I bet that's Dylan," she said as she hurried out of the room.

"Well, that was weird," Charlotte said as she followed me out of the room.

I agreed it was strange, but I would have to wait to ask more questions.

My mother had already cornered Dylan by the front door and was asking him a lot of questions.

"You'd better get a handle on that before he runs screaming from the house." Charlotte's gold bangle bracelets clanged together as she spoke with her hands.

I hurried over and stepped between them, interrupting their conversation. "How was your drive?" I looped my arm through Dylan's.

"It was great."

My dad popped inside from the back porch. "Nice to see you again, Dylan. Is everyone ready to eat?"

"Yes, we're starving." I led Dylan to the back porch where the aroma of burgers filled the air.

My father piled the plastic plates with food until they bent from the weight. Charlotte and Juliana sat on the chaise longue chairs, chatting away. What would everyone say if they knew ghosts were lounging on the porch with us?

Not a single cloud filled the brilliant blue sky. A slight breeze came in off the water and sea gulls looped high above the house. A perfect fall day.

After some chitchat while eating, my mother changed the subject. "So are there any new leads on the murder case?"

"Oh boy," Charlotte said.

Dylan smiled. "Now I know where Cookie gets it from."

My mother seemed unfazed by his comment and stared at him wide-eyed waiting for an answer.

"We're working on it." He took a bite of his burger.

"I don't think he wants to discuss the case, Mom." I said.

Dylan hid his smile behind his napkin, his way to

thank me for stopping her from questioning him further.

By the time we'd finished the food and put everything away, Dylan had to leave. I was ready to drive back too, but my mother insisted that I spend the night. He looked disappointed. I knew why. Earlier, he had mentioned finishing our dance.

"I think you should go home and dance with Dylan." Charlotte wiggled her eyebrows.

I wanted that too, but I also wanted to ask my mother more questions about the psychic.

Dylan and I had just walked to the front door when my phone rang. At first, I didn't recognize the number then realized it was Ken calling. I preferred that Dylan not hear the conversation and ignored it.

Dylan looked at me. "Aren't you going to answer it?"

I waved my hand. "I can take the call later."

He looked at me suspiciously.

"You're not a good liar, Cookie," Charlotte said. "He's a detective, remember? He can read people."

Yeah, I didn't need the reminder. I was already nervous enough. I hurried him out the door so that I could hear what Ken had to say. I hoped that he had found out something good. I said good-bye to Dylan and then checked my voicemail. Ken wanted me to call him back right away. That meant it was something good. I called him back.

He answered right away. "Hi Cookie. Can you meet me tonight?"

"Can it wait until tomorrow?" I asked, looking over my shoulder at my mother.

"It really can't."

"Okay. I'm at my parents' house on Tybee. I can be there in a little bit." I hung up after we set the time and place to meet.

I wouldn't be able to get my mother to tell me any more about the psychic. I would have to find out more later. After saying good-bye to my parents, I pointed the Buick in the direction of Sugar Creek.

My mother was still waving good-bye as if I was going off to war and she'd possibly never see me again. It was no secret that she had a flair for the dramatics.

Dylan would wonder why I'd returned.

Chapter 22

Charlotte's Tips for a Fashionable Afterlife

❦

*It only takes seconds to get ready
in the morning. This leaves you time
for many other things . . . like solving murders.*

Ken called and said he couldn't meet with me
after all. He'd thought he had a witness to the
murder, but it hadn't panned out. Of course I was
disappointed. A witness might have had the clue that
we needed.

I was back to searching for the cat's true identity.
Since I was so close to Sugar Creek, I called Heather
to see if she could go with me back to Fatima's. I
picked her up, and we drove straight to the psychic's
shop.

Inside, the smell of incense and candles hit me
in the face. Fatima was nowhere in sight. As I moved
toward the middle of the room, she popped up
beside me.

"Oh, for heaven's sake. Why does she do that?" Charlotte clutched her chest.

It had scared me and Juliana too. Heather was off checking out the inventory.

"It's nice to see you again." Fatima set the book she'd had in her hand on the nearby table.

I was surprised that she remembered me. I hated to keep coming in and never buying anything. All I ever wanted was for her to give me information.

"What can I do for you?" she asked.

I picked up a candle and sniffed. "Actually, I wanted to ask you a couple more questions."

She smiled. "Sure."

"I really need the information about someone who was in here"—I took a big breath—"for a séance."

"I'm sorry, but I can't give out that information. I've told you that before. It's just not right to violate someone's privacy."

"Yes, I understand, but this is important."

She shook her head. "I just can't."

What should I do? How can I convince her? I tried for a look of deep concern and said, "You see, I think my mother was here."

"And?"

"It's important that I find out. Can you just tell me if she was here?" I watched her furrow her brow and knew I had her interest.

She stared at me. "What did you want to know?" she asked in a lower voice as if someone might hear.

Heather moved closer to me. As far as I could tell, we were the only ones in the shop.

"My mother had your card. That's what made me think she was here. She doesn't come to Savannah often. I wondered what she did when she was here."

Fatima shook her head as she straightened the books on the display. "There's no way for me to know. A lot of people come in here. I don't get everybody's names."

Yes, I supposed that would be the case.

"Cookie, this isn't going to work. Plus, you're stressing this woman out. Let's just go. Leave her alone." Charlotte attempted to pull on my arm, but all I felt was a cold breeze.

I wasn't finished just yet. The woman didn't appear all that stressed to me. I suddenly remembered the photo of my mother. "Wait. I have a picture." I opened my red clutch and pulled out the photo. It showed my mother by the beach, holding up the hem of her skirt so it wouldn't get wet. In her other hand she held her sandals. "Here she is." I handed the photo to Fatima.

She studied it.

"Do you remember her?" I asked.

A look of recognition appeared on Fatima's face as she handed the photo back to me. "Yes, she was here . . . when the cat appeared. The one you asked about before. She was trying to contact your grandmother."

My eyes widened. "Why would she do that?" She'd never mentioned it to me.

"Why didn't she ask me to do it?" Heather wondered.

Well, Heather had admitted a long time ago that

she couldn't talk to ghosts . . . but my mother didn't know that.

"That's why I like to keep this private," Fatima said.

Thoughts flooded my mind. Things were starting to make sense about the cat . . . but—I shook my head. It couldn't be. It was impossible. I didn't even know how to ask. I needed time to wrap my mind around what I was thinking. If I was wrong, I would look certifiable.

"Are you okay?" Fatima asked, breaking me out of my thoughts.

"Oh, yes, I was just thinking about why she came."

"She was probably just curious. She'll talk to you about it when she's ready."

"I suppose you're right. Thanks for the info." I placed the photo back in my purse.

Fatima touched my hand. "Please, don't tell her I told you."

"You have my word." How was I going to let my mother know that I knew?

Heather and I walked out of the shop. Juliana and Charlotte were right behind us.

"Why didn't your mother come to me?" Heather asked again in a pouty voice.

"You can't talk to ghosts, remember?" I said.

"She doesn't know that." Heather shifted her tote bag to her other shoulder.

"She sure wouldn't have gotten her money's worth."

The corner of Charlotte's mouth twisted up on one side.

"What do I do now?" I asked.

"I guess you'll have to wait for her to talk to you about it," Heather said.

"Yes, you don't want to nag her about it," Charlotte said. "That would be annoying."

We got into my car and headed back to Sugar Creek. I wanted to share my thoughts with everyone but was nervous they'd think I'd lost my mind.

Charlotte leaned forward, propping her arms against the back of the front seat. "Cookie, I don't know how to tell you this . . . but did you ever stop to think that the cat might be your grandmother?"

I swerved, throwing everybody sideways and almost wrecking the car into the ditch. Everyone screamed while I got the car straightened out.

"Cookie, what's the matter with you?" Charlotte asked while straightening her hair.

"Sorry. It's just that I thought I was the only one thinking that."

"What did she say?" Heather asked.

"Charlotte thinks Wind Song is my grandmother. The thought crossed my mind too. How would that be possible?"

Heather smoothed Burt's Bees lip balm across her lips as if this was just an ordinary, everyday conversation. "When they had the séance, your grandmother found the physical body she needed to stay here on earth."

I raised an eyebrow. "A cat?"

"Not just any cat." Charlotte leaned forward again. "A gorgeous cat."

If my grandmother were to ever come back as a cat, it would definitely be one who looked just like Wind Song. I couldn't let myself believe that my grandmother was inside the cat. It just couldn't be possible . . . could it?

Chapter 23

Cookie's Savvy Tips for Vintage Shopping

*Everyone can benefit from a fun piece
of vintage clothing in their closet.*

The next day, I closed the shop early. We'd agreed
to try a séance. I had to admit it was mostly my idea
at first, but Charlotte, Juliana, and Heather went
along easily. I wondered how it would work taking
ghosts with me to a séance. Usually, spirits were
invited after the séance was started, not before.

For the special event, I wore my Corey Lynn
Calter black and white houndstooth dress. It had a
strapless bodice, which was boned for a structured
corset-style fit. The waist was fitted and surrounded
with a grosgrain ribbon. The skirt was full. I was
hoping it would turn out to be my lucky dress. Since
it was slightly cool, I'd covered up with my favorite
black Dior cardigan. The delicate rhinestone buttons
reminded me of diamonds.

We were all in my Buick barreling down the road toward Savannah to meet Fatima. Of course, Wind Song had insisted on coming too. She was just one of the girls and wanted to be included.

I pulled into a spot and parked out front. Not knowing what to expect, I was anxious with anticipation. "Do you think she'll mind if I bring Wind Song in?" I asked.

"She'd probably like to see her again, but maybe you should keep her in the carrier," Heather said.

We all filed into the shop.

I placed the carrier on the floor. "I'll be right back, Wind Song." I walked over to the area set up for the séance. In the center was a table covered with a white cloth. Chairs circled it. "I guess this is where it's going to happen."

Heather released a deep breath. "Yeah, I guess this is it."

The lights were dim. The smell of incense filled the air and candles cast an eerie glow, flickering around the room.

"This is kind of spooky," I said.

"There's nothing to be afraid of." Heather didn't sound convinced.

Fatima came into the room, instructing us with a wave of her hand. "Please have a seat around the table."

Heather and I each pulled out a chair and sat.

Nervous thoughts crashed in my brain. *This might be a good time to tell Fatima that I brought ghosts with me. Then again, she might not be happy about that. Perhaps I should keep that part a secret. Can she sense they're here? I swear she looked right in their direction.*

Stop! I told myself silently. "Is three people enough?" I asked.

"That's fine," Fatima said, motioning for us to take her hands.

We held hands and placed them on top of the table.

"Let's start," she said.

I closed my eyes as she started asking for protection and light. Then she began calling out to any spirits who might be with us.

Of course Charlotte started goofing around and dancing. "I'm here. I'm here. Talk to me. Talk to me."

Juliana giggled.

"I'm sensing a spirit," Fatima said. "A female."

I glanced at Charlotte.

In a quiet voice, Fatima said, "She's a bit high strung and loves attention."

Charlotte placed her hands on her hips. "Well who doesn't love attention? There's nothing wrong with that."

I laughed. I couldn't help myself.

Fatima looked at me and then continued. "We would like to talk with the spirit who entered Wind Song."

Nothing happened. Everything remained quiet. Even Charlotte was behaving. I was quickly becoming discouraged but wasn't quite ready to give up yet.

Suddenly a loud bang sounded from somewhere in the room. We all looked at each other and then the wind picked up. The candles flickered and the next thing I knew, they all went out. Everything was dark in the room.

"I had nothing to do with that," Charlotte said from somewhere in the darkness.

"The spirit is here," Fatima said.

How would I know?

Suddenly the candles lit again and I knew we weren't alone in the room. Wind Song was sitting at the table with us.

"How did you get out of your carrier?" I reached over and picked her up. "I'm sorry about that." I took Wind Song back to her carrier, placed her inside, and closed the door. "Now, Wind Song, we're almost done. Stay put, okay?"

She meowed in protest. I went back to the table. "Sorry again."

"That's okay. Let's continue, shall we?"

I took my seat again and held hands with Fatima and Heather. The candles flickered through several more minutes of Fatima's questions. When nothing happened, she decided we should end our attempts. The only ghost I'd gotten a chance to talk to was Charlotte. I had enough of that twenty-four/seven.

"You have two spirits with you," Fatima said. "They're with you all the time, but they won't give me their names."

I smirked. "That sounds typical."

I wasn't quite ready to tell her that I had ghosts following me all the time and I was well aware of who they are. I thanked Fatima for her time and grabbed Wind Song's carrier as we headed out the door.

"Well, I have to hand it to her, she's better than Heather. At least she detected our presence, but that little remark about me being high strung . . . she was way off base with that one."

"Yes, how could she have ever detected that you were a drama queen?" I said.

Since we were already in Savannah, I knew I had to pay my parents a visit. My mother might not be so happy when I started asking questions.

We made the short drive to my parents' house and pulled up right in front. It was as if my mother sensed me because as soon as I stepped foot on the driveway, she opened the door.

"Cookie, why didn't you call first? I'm so excited to see you."

"Now, your mother, she's high strung," Charlotte said.

My mother hugged me and then moved over to Heather. "Heather, I just love your shirt. Did you make it yourself?"

Heather beamed. "Yes, I did with all natural dye."

"Y'all can discuss your uses for hemp later. Let's go inside." Picking up the cat carrier, I ushered them into the house.

I unlatched the carrier door and Wind Song strolled out.

"Come to the kitchen. I have special treats for y'all," my mother said.

"Yum. More of those chickpea cookies," I said.

"Don't be sassy, Cookie," she warned with a wave of her hand.

"That sounds fantastic." Heather's eyes lit up.

"I swear I think you two were switched at birth," Charlotte said.

I kind of agreed with her on that one.

My mother poured glasses of soy milk and set out the cookies. "So what brings you by?"

I noticed she kept glancing over at the cat. "Is something wrong?"

She waved her hand. "Oh, it's just that I think your father might be allergic to the cat."

"That's the first I've heard of it," I said.

"It's a new development." She took a bite of a cookie.

"Is he here?" I asked.

Mom shook her head. "No, but he'll be home soon."

Something made me suspicious. I didn't think she was being truthful. "If he comes in, I can take the cat back outside."

Was she scared of the cat? I couldn't understand why. She'd never been in the past.

Heather was busy eating the cookies and drinking her milk.

My mother sat in the chair across from her. "You have to give me your method for making that shirt."

I displayed a timeout signal with my hands. "Wait a minute. We're not done talking. I have some questions first."

She wasn't going to change the subject that easily. It was as if she was avoiding my questions. Did she know what I was about to ask?

My mother grimaced. "Well, what's your question, Cookie?"

"You went to the psychic in Savannah. I want to know why." I didn't take my eyes off her.

She shifted in the chair, clearly uncomfortable. "I told you it was just a group of friends. We were just having fun."

"I think there's more to it than that. Heather knows the psychic and we have reason to believe that you were trying to contact Grandma Pearl."

My mother's face drained of blood and she shifted again as if she might take off in a sprint. After some thought and a deep breath she stayed put. "Okay. Yes, I tried to contact your grandmother."

Wind Song meowed.

Could I really tell my mother what I suspected had happened?

Chapter 24

Charlotte's Tips for a Fashionable Afterlife

Have a design in mind?
You can design clothing
even if you can't sketch or sew.

The next morning, I slipped into my Betty Hanson 1970s wool skirt. A wrap style with a wooden button closure, it hit just above the knees. For a glam touch, I matched it with a black wool short-sleeved sweater that had oversized sequin buttons down the front. My black wedge heels finished the outfit. As hard as it was, I wanted to keep things as normal as possible in my life.

I opened the shop right on time and worked through the morning, anticipating what I might find at the estate sale I planned to visit later. Although they were usually scheduled for weekends, I'd noticed one advertised in the newspaper scheduled to open for a brief "preview" later today. Searching for vintage treasures always relaxed me, and I needed that more than ever.

"We don't have time for this, Cookie. We have to solve the murder," Charlotte said as we left for the sale.

"If I don't find more stock for my shop, I won't have the means to do anything, Charlotte."

"She's right, Charlotte. Cookie can't stop her life just to solve this case," Juliana said.

Charlotte quit pushing. "You're right. I don't know what I was thinking. Business always comes first."

She was just trying to make me feel bad.

We all got in the car and headed across town to the sale. Charlotte was chattering away about some dress she'd seen in the window in town and how she thought that I should have it.

"I suppose I could go by and take a look at it later," I said.

"It would look phenomenal on you," Charlotte said. "You have to get it for your next date with Dylan."

"But I wear vintage, remember?" I said.

"You always say you like to incorporate new with the old."

I made the next right turn. "Okay, I guess I should follow my own advice."

It was a pleasant day. I was looking forward to leisurely sorting through the items for sale. I had my fingers crossed that I'd find something fabulous. Lately, I'd had my eye out for some great Louis Vuitton or Gucci. So far nothing great had turned up, but I held out hope. I pulled up to the two-story brick home and shoved the car into park.

Charlotte peered at the house. "Not bad. You might find something good."

"It's a beautiful home," Juliana said.

We got out of the car and headed to the door. It was already open and other people had stepped inside. I had hoped to be one of the first, but that didn't always work out when I had to wait on ghosts. Charlotte had taken her time getting ready this morning and that hadn't improved any this afternoon. What took her so long was beyond me. All she had to do was think about her outfit and it appeared. Unlike me. I had to plan my clothing choices well in advance.

Sorting through the hanging blouses, I managed to find a beautiful black Dior, but that was all on that rack. I spotted some handbags on a table across the room and made a mad dash like a baseball player running to home plate. Unfortunately, I found nothing I wanted.

I wandered around a bit more but found nothing else. However, I did feel like someone was watching me . . . like the time when I had met Charlotte at her estate sale. Surely there wasn't another ghost around. I didn't think I could handle more than two at a time.

I peeked across the room and thought for sure I'd seen Regina walk into the hallway. *What is she doing here?* I hurried across the room to catch up with her.

Juliana followed me.

"Was that your Aunt Regina?"

"It looked like her, but she moved quickly and I didn't get a good glance."

"I didn't know Regina could move that fast," Charlotte said.

Reaching the hallway, I spotted Regina and moved toward her. "Regina?"

At first, she didn't turn around and look at me.

I tapped her on the shoulder. "Regina? What are you doing here?"

Finally, she turned around. "Oh, Cookie, what are you doing here?" Regina asked with wide eyes as if she was surprised.

"Well, I go to estate sales a lot, Regina. Remember, I own the vintage shop?"

"Oh, yes, yes," she said with a wave of her hand. "Now that you mention it, I do remember that."

Charlotte folded her arms across her chest. "I don't believe her. She knows what she's doing here. Did she follow you?"

"She has no reason to follow Cookie," Juliana said.

"Oh, you're so naïve and sweet," Charlotte said.

"So what are you doing here, Regina?" I asked again.

"I was just looking for some clothing."

She did have a blue sweater draped across her arm, so I supposed that could have been the truth.

"Well, I must be going now. It was nice seeing you. Ta-ta." Regina hurried out of the hallway.

"That was strange," Charlotte said.

"I told you she was eccentric," Juliana said.

"Whatever the reason, I think I've seen enough. I'm going to pay for this blouse," I said.

"Good. I'm ready to go," Charlotte said.

After paying for my purchase, I headed out with the ghosts. Before I hopped into the car, I looked around. "I don't see Regina anywhere."

We got into the car and I started it up.

"I didn't even know she drove," Juliana said as we headed down the street.

"She probably shouldn't," Charlotte said. "Where to now?"

"I need to go grocery shopping. I'll just leave the Dior blouse in the car."

"Good," Charlotte said. "We're in a hurry."

"We are?" I asked.

"Sure. The sooner you're done with this, the sooner we can get back to solving the crime." Charlotte was practically obsessed with finding out who'd murdered Juliana.

Once you're murdered, you kind of make it your life's mission to help others, I guessed.

We pulled into the grocery store parking lot and headed inside.

"No fattening stuff," Charlotte warned.

"Yeah right."

I'd do whatever I wanted, although I did want to keep the junk to a minimum. I liked to eat healthy, but not because Charlotte told me to. I had enough of those warnings from my mother. I didn't need Charlotte doing it too.

Chapter 25

Cookie's Savvy Tips for Vintage Shopping

**If the vintage garment
you fell in love with doesn't fit,
don't be afraid to have it tailored.**

I headed down the grocery aisle, putting a few items in my cart. As I rounded a corner, Regina popped up from the next aisle. I stopped in my tracks. Charlotte practically ran right through me, she'd been following so close.

"What are you doing?" Charlotte brushed off the invisible dirt she thought she'd attracted from running into me.

"Regina was just here."

"I'm so sorry, Cookie," Juliana said.

I shook my head. "It's not your fault."

Pushing the cart down the aisle as fast as I could, I finally came to the end. I made a sharp left turn and pushed the cart around to the next aisle, thinking that Regina would be there. She'd already reached the end.

"She moves fast," Charlotte said.

"She's trying to hide from me," I said. "I don't know what she's up to, but something's going on."

Regina went around to the next aisle.

"Regina," I called out, pushing the cart again and following her. I didn't find her when I reached the next aisle—the canned food aisle.

"It's like she disappeared," Juliana said.

I stopped and looked around, but didn't see her.

"Maybe she's hiding." I looked up and around in hopes of catching her. Had she climbed the shelves to get away from me?

"Whatever. Maybe she just needed to get groceries. It could be a coincidence." Juliana peeked around the corner of the aisle.

"Probably," I said.

I paid for my items and then headed out to the parking lot. Part of me expected to see Regina out there, waiting for me. As I pushed the cart to my car, I realized she was nowhere around. I placed the items in my trunk and then headed for home.

"So what about looking at that dress now?" Charlotte asked.

I pulled into my driveway. "Well, maybe later."

"Oh, what are you making for dinner?" she asked.

"I'm not cooking." I'd skipped lunch and was hungry. I grabbed the bags from the trunk.

"But you just went to the grocery."

"Yes, but I'm too hungry. I'll just drop the stuff off and then head over to Glorious Grits."

Charlotte grimaced, showing her feelings on that idea. "Again?"

I quickly put the groceries away and headed back into town. I wanted to try some of those specials Dixie had said she'd added to the menu. Once I found a spot to park, I hurried toward the diner. I walked in and took the first booth by the window. It was still a little early so not many people had arrived yet. Dixie spotted me and waved that she'd be right over.

"Does she work all the time?" Charlotte asked.

"Just like you used to," I said.

"Maybe she should take a little vacation," Juliana said.

"You'd have an easier time convincing her of that than I would."

"But she can't see me."

"Exactly," I said.

As soon as Dixie came over, I placed my order and waited for her to bring back water. A few other people had arrived so the room was starting to fill up.

"This is so sad," Charlotte said.

"What's sad?" I asked.

"The fact that you're eating dinner all alone. It's so pitiful."

I grabbed a napkin in anticipation of my mouth-watering food. "I don't mind eating alone. It allows me time to reflect. Besides, I'm not eating alone. I have you two."

"Yes, the other people can't see that though. It just makes you look sad and lonely."

"Well, you're in luck. Here comes Heather. I'm sure she'll eat with me."

"That's not much better," Charlotte said.

"Well, you'll just have to take what you can get," I said with a smile.

Heather slid into the booth. "What's happening?"

"I ordered the new special. You should try it." I handed her a menu.

She read it and quickly decided. "Sounds delicious. I think I will." She placed her order with Dixie.

I filled Heather in on seeing Regina at the estate sale and at the grocery store.

"That is strange, but I suppose it could really be a coincidence like Juliana said." Heather took a sip of water.

"Actually"—I tapped the tabletop—"I hope it is just a coincidence."

Heather's eyes widened.

"What is it?" I asked.

She pointed out the window. "I don't think it was a coincidence. I just saw you-know-who walk by. She was looking in here."

"Regina just walked by?" I turned in my seat.

"I'm pretty sure it was her," Heather said.

"You can't let that behavior go unchecked," Charlotte said.

I wasn't quite sure what I could do.

"You should just ask her what she's doing . . . especially if she's going to be this wacky. You shouldn't hesitate to ask her," Heather said.

I wasn't sure if I was up for another confrontation just yet.

* * *

By the time Heather and I finished our dinner, it was early evening.

"I have to head out," she said. "Unfortunately, I have some errands to run for my mother." She stood up from the table.

I hugged her good-bye. "I'll call you later."

Charlotte was still badgering me to go look at the dress so I relented and headed down to the little shop around the corner. The place really did have beautiful things and I occasionally purchased something there. I wasn't a complete vintage snob. All clothing was beautiful in my eyes—fabrics, the colors, and designs all made me swoon. Adding extras like jewelry, shoes, and handbags were like the cherry on top of a sundae.

I popped into the place and did a quick scan.

Charlotte pointed to the window display. "There it is. That's the one right there."

It was a beautiful red dress and she was right. It was stunning. The boutique's owner wasn't there so I talked with her part-time employee Patricia.

"Can I get something for you?" she asked.

"I'd like to see that dress please." I pointed to the one in the window.

"I think it might be your size. Would you like to try it on?"

"Um"—I glanced at Charlotte—"yes."

Patricia stepped into the display area, took the dress off the mannequin, and handed it to me.

I headed toward the dressing room.

"You should always try the clothes on," Charlotte said.

After slipping into the dress and getting Charlotte's approval, I made the purchase.

"Dylan is going to love you in the dress. I bet Ken wouldn't mind either." Charlotte winked.

"Okay, now you're just making me blush."

"Did you say something?" Patricia asked.

I took the bag from her outstretched hand. "Oh no, I was just observing how much I like the dress." I was really slipping lately, talking to the ghosts in front of other people. Surely people would think I was crazy and word would spread around Sugar Creek quickly.

As I turned to leave, I spotted someone walk past the window. Sure enough, it was Regina . . . again. I knew for sure it was no coincidence. I turned back to Patricia. "Did you see her?"

"The woman who just walked past? Yes, I did. She's been standing at the window watching you the whole time you were in here."

"Okay, that's a little creepy," Juliana admitted.

"You have to find out what she's doing," Charlotte said.

Maybe I should go ahead and ask Regina what she wants. Does she want to talk to me and just doesn't know how to approach the subject? If she wants the hat, I can't help her with that.

"Thanks again, Patricia." I hurried out of the store and onto the sidewalk, hoping that I would spot Regina. "Do you see her?" I asked Juliana and Charlotte.

They shook their heads.

"No, she's nowhere around. Maybe she's headed back to her house," Charlotte said.

"I suppose I could give it a shot."

I climbed back into the car and headed over to Regina's house.

She was walking in the door just as I pulled up.

I hurried out of the car to catch her. "Regina," I called out.

She didn't turn around, but I was almost certain she knew I was there. My car was so loud I was more than a little noticeable. I couldn't sneak up on anyone. Regina closed the door before I could reach her.

"Why did she do that?" Juliana said.

"I don't know if she's just being rude or she didn't see you," Charlotte said.

"She always acts that way," Juliana said.

I rang the bell. Surely she wouldn't ignore that. I waited, but she didn't answer. I pushed the bell again and called out to her. Still she didn't answer.

"Regina, I know you're there. I just saw you." I couldn't make her come to the door. It didn't seem fair for her to follow me around and leave me wondering what she wanted and then ignore me. "I suppose she doesn't want to talk."

"Maybe by following her it will stop her from following you," Charlotte said.

I walked off the porch and got back into my car. I looked over at the house to see if she was watching me. It surprised me that she wasn't looking out. Maybe she would talk to Ken and tell him why she was following me. If she needed help, I wanted to help her.

I gave one last glance at the house and then pulled away from the curb.

"That was completely unsuccessful," Charlotte said.

"Yeah, you win some and you lose some," I said as I made the next left turn and headed home.

Chapter 26

Charlotte's Tips for a Fashionable Afterlife

*You can try new styles
without worrying how you look.*

The next day was uneventful except for Dylan's
phone call asking me out again.

For tonight's date I would wear the red dress
Charlotte had insisted I purchase. I'd just taken it out
of the closet when my cell rang.

"It's Ken," Charlotte said as she peered down at
my phone.

I raced over and grabbed it. "Hello."

"Good evening. I hope I didn't catch you at a bad
time." His sweet Southern accent could send a shiver
through anyone's soul.

He really is a doll. I grinned. "No, not at all." I
looked over at the clock on my nightstand. I had fifteen minutes before Dylan would be there. Why did

I feel so strange talking to Ken and thinking of Dylan? Was it because Ken was so kind?

I didn't like what I was thinking. Charlotte had put all those troubling thoughts into my mind.

She and Juliana stood in front of me, anxiously waiting for me to tell them what Ken said. Charlotte motioned for me to put the call on speakerphone, but there was no way I would do that. I'd learned the hard way that wasn't such a good idea. Anytime anyone mentioned something about the case, she would insist that I follow up on the lead right away.

"I'm calling because I have information about Victor," Ken said.

"Really? What did you find out?" My question caught Charlotte and Juliana's attention.

"Victor served time for burglary," Ken said.

"When?" I asked.

"What's he saying?" Charlotte leaned closer, trying to hear.

"He was released last year."

Why wouldn't Dylan tell me this? He had to know. Was he just trying to protect me? That would explain why he thought Victor had broken into my shop.

"Do you know what the charges were?"

"He held up a store with another guy. His defense was that he didn't know the guy was robbing the place and claimed he wasn't involved."

"I guess the jury didn't believe him."

"He got a reduced sentence because of it though,"

Ken said. "I'd like to discuss this with you more. Are you free tonight?"

I felt bad telling him no. "Actually, I do have plans."

"What about tomorrow? I could meet you for lunch."

"I have some time around one."

"Things are starting to turn around for you in the love department." Charlotte winked.

How did she know this had anything to do with love?

"So is it a date?" Ken asked.

Thank goodness Charlotte hadn't heard that. Another reason why I didn't want the call on speakerphone.

"Sure, I'll see you then."

As soon as I hung up, she wanted to know what happened so I told her about Victor.

"You're meeting Ken for lunch?" Charlotte asked.

There was no way to keep that from her.

"If I have time. Things may come up."

"What could possibly come up?"

"Something with the murder."

"That's unlikely." Charlotte clapped her hands. "This is fantastic for the case, Cookie. Tonight you can ask Dylan everything and tomorrow you can have Ken follow up on what you learn."

"That's kind of using both of them, isn't it?" I asked.

"Don't rain on our parade," Charlotte said as she gestured toward Juliana.

She was right. I needed to solve the case. Plus, after being shot at, it could be a life or death situation. Sure it looked as if Charlotte was having fun as a ghost, but I didn't want to check out just yet. I still had too much to do. I didn't feel as if it was my time to go.

Ten minutes to get dressed seemed plenty of time, considering I'd already selected my outfit. I wore the new red dress and finished it with a pair of Louboutins. I spun around. "How do I look?"

"Like you just stepped out of a magazine," Juliana said.

"You need a little more lip gloss," Charlotte said.

I studied my reflection. "Maybe I could use just a little more." I swiped it across my lips and then the doorbell rang.

"He's here!" Charlotte yelled.

I grabbed my bag and hurried to the door with the ghosts right behind me. Wind Song was already sitting beside the door when I reached the hallway. It was as if they were seeing me off for prom. The problem was the ghosts were going along on this date as if they were my chaperones.

I opened the door. Dylan stood in front of me. He was wearing a black suit and a light blue shirt with a dark blue tie. It wasn't vintage, but he still look gorgeous.

"You look beautiful." Dylan leaned in and kissed my cheek.

"I was just about to say the same to you. Well,

handsome instead of beautiful." I loved that he always took the time to compliment me.

"Are you ready to go? I have something special planned."

"Oh, this should be exciting. I love surprises," Charlotte said.

I grabbed my keys. "I've had a lot of surprises lately."

"Was that a comment about me?" Charlotte placed her hands on her hips. "Because I can't help it if you have psychic abilities."

"Well, I didn't ask for the ability either." I looked at her.

We froze when we realized that I'd just responded to her in front of Dylan. I wasn't surprised actually. It had become harder with each passing day to remember that he couldn't see the ghosts.

He was looking at me oddly.

"You have to say something." Charlotte wiped her forehead.

"Tell him you were talking to the cat," Juliana said.

I could use the cat as my excuse, but what I said didn't really make sense. I wasn't thinking of something quick enough. I reached down and picked up the cat anyway. "I didn't ask for the ability to love this cat so much." I kissed Wind Song and then placed her on the floor.

"Nice try, Cookie. Try not to mess this up any more tonight," Charlotte said. "He'll leave you at the restaurant."

Dylan quirked an eyebrow.

"See, he's fine," Juliana said.

"He probably thinks she has a screw loose." Charlotte stepped around Dylan onto the porch.

She and Juliana followed us out to the car.

"We should drive my car. The weather is so nice tonight, we can ride with the top down." I handed Dylan the keys. "Would you like to drive?"

He stared at me for a moment. "I'd love to."

"You don't let anyone drive your car," Charlotte said. "Plus, what about your hair?"

Dylan slipped behind the wheel. It was strange seeing someone else on the driver's side. Even weirder to be on the passenger side. I released a deep breath and told myself that I could do this. After all, he had plenty of experience driving. With a crank of the engine, we headed out and away from downtown Sugar Creek.

"When are you going to tell me where we're going?" I asked after a couple miles.

He used the signal to make a left turn into a gravel parking lot. "We're here."

The little café was out of the way and set back from the road a bit. The building was just a tiny white wood house that looked as if it had room for only a couple people at once. Pine and oak trees surrounded the place making it seem even more isolated.

"Have you ever eaten here?" When I shook my head, he said, "I think you'll love it."

"This is his surprise? I thought he was taking you for a gourmet meal. I suppose we can forgive him because he's so handsome, but still." Charlotte had her own ideas on fancy and romantic.

Dylan parked the car then opened the door for me. I straightened my new red dress so that it wouldn't have wrinkles. Now that I saw the place I felt over-dressed.

The young hostess greeted us and then sat us at a table in the middle of the room. Of course it wasn't far from the exit, the restrooms, or the kitchen. With a space so small everything was near. The walls were covered with pictures of different locations in Sugar Creek. I wondered if my boutique was pictured anywhere on the wall.

"You should try the spaghetti," Dylan said as he peeked over the top of the menu.

Charlotte placed the back of her hand to her forehead as if she'd faint. "Spaghetti? What's next? Hot dogs and tater tots?"

Hey, I liked tater tots. They had the best ones at Sonic, along with the hot dogs. Charlotte just wanted to go to some fancy French place.

The waitress took our order. As I sipped on my red wine I contemplated how to approach the subject of the murder.

"Just come right out and ask him," Charlotte said as if she'd read my mind.

Dylan studied my face for a moment. "I know what you're about to say. No talking about the case. Tonight is all about us."

"While that is romantic, it is highly disappointing." Charlotte paced around the table, almost bumping into the waitress when she brought our food.

The waitress looked around as if she'd sensed something or someone. It was the cold breeze that Charlotte left everywhere she went that the waitress probably felt.

"It's okay, Charlotte. They need their alone time." Juliana pulled on Charlotte's arm, dragging her away.

As we ate our meals, Dylan insisted I fill him in on recent events in my life . . . anything that didn't involve murder. Actually, it was kind of hard to come up with something. Finally, I told him about my plans for the fall festival. He told me about his search for a vintage car. He wanted to restore one. It was exciting to find out that had been a dream of his since he was a teenager.

I'd just finished my last bite of spaghetti when raised voices captured my attention. Peeking over Dylan's shoulder, I noticed the waitress arguing with someone. I wasn't expecting Regina to be the person on the other end of that argument. "It's looks like there's a problem." I pointed toward them.

Dylan peered over his shoulder and then stood from the table. He crossed the room and joined the ladies who were still arguing. "What seems to be the problem?"

The waitress pointed at Regina. "She took my tip from this table."

Dylan looked at Regina. "Is that true?"

Regina stiffened. "Absolutely not. I would never do such a thing."

"Then where is the money?" the waitress asked.

"I don't know what happened to your money."

I moved a little closer. "Is that the money on the floor?"

A few crumpled dollars lay on the floor next to Regina's foot. Everyone peered down.

Dylan picked up the cash. "How much was it?"

"Seven dollars," the waitress said. "I noticed when the customer left it, I just hadn't had the chance to pick it up yet."

Dylan counted the money and then handed it to the waitress.

"I have no idea how that got down there," Regina said.

"Well, it was on the table behind her, so I guess it just walked over there." The waitress glared at Regina.

Dylan led Regina away from the table. "Maybe it's time you left, Regina. Do you have a way home?"

She jerked her arm away from Dylan. "Don't touch me." She stormed out the door.

Since I was standing near the door, I peeked outside to see where she went. I spotted her getting into a car. I was almost sure the driver of that car was Hunter and wondered out loud, "Why would she leave with Hunter?"

Dylan stood beside me, looking out the window. "Are you sure?"

"Almost sure."

Not only had she left with Hunter, but someone who looked a lot like Victor was in the backseat. Were they involved in something together?

We decided against dessert and Dylan paid the bill. He held the door open for me and we walked out into the cool night air. An expanse of stars twinkled in the sky like diamonds.

"This wasn't the romantic ending I'd hoped for," Charlotte said from over my shoulder.

Apparently they'd been waiting outside the door for us. I'd have to ask if they'd seen Hunter and Victor waiting for Regina.

Chapter 27

Cookie's Savvy Tips for Vintage Shopping

❦

*Make sure to check if the fabric
is in good condition.
If it is ready to fall apart, you will waste money
and be unhappy with the item.*

In my dream, I heard ringing . . . several rings.
Charlotte managed to wake me by yelling at me to
answer the phone and I finally realized my cell was
ringing. I grabbed the phone from the nightstand.
Dylan was calling early. I wondered if something
was wrong.

"Did I wake you?" he asked when I picked up.

"No, I was just getting up."

"You are such a liar," Charlotte said as she sat on
the edge of the bed next to me.

I was glad Dylan couldn't hear her comments. "Is
something wrong?" I asked him.

"Maybe he just wanted to hear your voice,"

Charlotte said as she studied her perfect French manicure.

"I've been thinking about what you asked last night," Dylan said.

"Which question was that? I asked several."

"I can take you to see the car, but you can't tell anyone." He lowered his voice as if someone might overhear.

I sat up in bed. "When can we go?"

"Oh, where are we going?" Charlotte sat up too.

I couldn't believe that I'd convinced him to let me have one more look at the contents in Juliana's car. That conversation had taken place in the car on the ride home. I was glad he'd agreed. Charlotte and Juliana hadn't seen anything unusual at the café. They'd seen Regina rush out, but that was all.

"Can you meet me in town in an hour? I can show you before work."

"I'll be there." I jumped up and rushed over to the closet.

After slipping into my outfit, I attempted to style my hair. When it wouldn't cooperate I just pulled it back into a ponytail. My coffee-color brown cigarette pants looked like they were from the 1950s, but they were a reproduction from the 1990s. Since they were covered with an with atomic print, my cream-colored cotton tank from the 1990s worked well. I paired the outfit with ivory flats.

"You look like you're going to high school in the fifties," Charlotte said.

"She's actually going on a dangerous mission," Juliana said.

I hoped it wasn't dangerous. I'd had enough of danger in the past few days. I grabbed my purse and keys. "Wind Song, I'll come back for you," I called as I opened the door.

She meowed loudly and ran out the door and over to the car.

"It looks as if she doesn't want to stay," Juliana said.

I glanced at my watch and back at the cat. "I suppose I have just enough time to drop you off before I meet Dylan." Without thinking, I opened the car door.

She jumped right into the front seat. She didn't wait to ride in her carrier.

"I'm not sure it's a good idea to ride without your carrier, Wind Song."

She meowed, but I went back inside for the carrier anyway. After getting her inside it, we took off for downtown.

I opened the boutique door, set the carrier on the floor, and let Wind Song out. I shut and locked the door behind me and ran to my car. I had ten minutes before it was time to meet Dylan.

I cruised through town to the lot where they kept the towed cars. Dylan was waiting in his car out front. He stepped out when I pulled up.

"This is exciting," Charlotte said as I shoved the car into park and turned off the ignition. "Just remember that we may find nothing."

"At least you can say you tried." Juliana slipped out of the car.

"Yes, you would always have wondered if you didn't give it a look." Charlotte kept pace next to me.

I walked up to Dylan. He leaned down and kissed me.

"At least he realizes there is always time for romance." Charlotte liked that.

Dylan peered around. "Remember, don't tell anyone about this."

It was a good thing Charlotte couldn't talk to anyone else. The news would be all over town.

Dylan unlocked the gate and we walked to the back of the lot. The ghosts walked with us, but when we neared the car, Juliana stopped.

"What's wrong?" Charlotte asked her.

She rubbed her arms. "It just brings back bad memories to see the car again."

"Well, that's understandable. How do you think I felt roaming around an empty mansion watching people drag all my belongings out? The Chanel . . . the Hermès. It was awful . . . but you move on and learn to deal with it."

I wished I could say something to Juliana and make her feel better, but Dylan was waiting for me.

Charlotte motioned over her shoulder at the Buick. "We'll wait in the car."

I hoped she was gentle with Juliana in spite of her abrasive style.

"You know we've already processed this car. Every inch has been searched," Dylan said with a wave of his hand.

"In other words, I'm wasting your time?"

"I didn't say that." Dylan opened the door. "I could tell by the look on your face that you wouldn't take no for an answer until you looked for yourself. I just don't want you to be disappointed when nothing turns up."

What could I say? The cat suggested that I look in the car?

Dylan stood guard outside the car as I poked in. I looked over at the driver's seat and a chill went down my spine. I didn't blame Juliana for not wanting to see the scene of the crime. It was disturbing to look at.

He had put doubt in my head. Of course I wouldn't find anything. I looked through the glove compartment, center console, and underneath the seats.

"Find anything?" Dylan asked.

"You know I haven't," I said over my shoulder.

I moved to the back seat and poked around, not finding anything. I hated to admit it, but this was a wasted trip. At least Dylan was nice enough to allow me to check out the car even though he knew I was wrong.

I was crawling across the seat when Dylan called out. "How's it going back there?"

"Cookie, for heaven's sake. That is some view." Charlotte had returned to the lot.

I moved quickly in the small space, bumping my head on the ceiling and popping off part of the seat. As I rubbed my head, I noticed something sticking out from behind the seat. Was it in some kind of hidden compartment? Of course. It had to be.

"Are you okay in there?" Dylan asked.

"Uh, just fine. I'm coming out." I reached in,

grabbed the vintage black bag, and climbed out of the backseat.

"What's that?" Dylan moved over to me.

"I found it in a secret compartment in the back-seat." I held up the bag.

"You're kidding."

I opened the bag, looked inside, then looked up at him. "If you were shocked that I found something, you'll be even more shocked to see what's in it." I handed him the bag.

He sifted through the cash.

"How much do you think is in there?"

"There must be twenty thousand here."

"That's a pretty good guess," I said.

"How did they miss this? How did the crime scene techs miss this?" Dylan said under his breath. He looked stunned.

Though I felt bad for their mistake, I was pretty proud of myself for the discovery. "Well, it was hidden. The purpose was obviously so no one would find it."

Dylan ran his hand through his hair. "I wish I knew if Juliana had hidden the money. Since she had it I assume she hid it there."

Even though it wasn't fair to Dylan, I was about to find out. I had a source that he would never know about.

I took the bag and looked inside again. "Do you think this is what the killer was looking for? It had to be, right? But why didn't he take it when he or she shot Juliana?"

Dylan shoved his hands into his pockets. "Likely it was because he couldn't find it."

Charlotte peered into the bag. "I could buy several nice handbags with that cash."

I ignored her and asked, "What happens now?"

Dylan grabbed the bag. "I'll take this to the station with me. We need to find out where the money came from. And we need to go over this car again."

"Will the persons who went through the car get in trouble?" I asked.

"Since it was hidden, no, I guess not."

"Whew. I'm glad. I don't want to be responsible for getting someone fired."

Dylan smiled at that then shook his head. "I still can't believe you found it."

"She has a natural knack for sleuthing," Charlotte said.

Juliana had obviously stayed in the Buick. I couldn't wait to ask her about it. Dylan and I walked back to the front.

He unlocked the gate. We stepped through, he relocked it, then placed the bag in his car. "I'll call you as soon as I find out anything." He stood by the door, waiting until I was safely in my car.

It was nice that he was finally including me. After all, I had helped the case a lot. I should be included. I climbed into my car and Charlotte immediately started talking about what I found.

My thoughts were jumbled as I started the car and drove off. It would make sense that Victor would have had cash since he liked to rob people. Did he give it to Hunter to hide? Hunter's grandmother had said he was looking for something that he'd hidden.

"Were Hunter and Victor working together?" Charlotte asked suddenly.

She was right. That had to be it.

"I still don't think Hunter is capable of doing anything like that," Juliana said.

I looked at her in the rearview mirror. "Maybe he didn't know. Maybe Victor was just using him."

She agreed. "That makes a lot more sense to me."

"So you don't know when they could have hidden the money or how the secret section got there?" I pulled up in front of It's Vintage Y'all and cut the engine.

"Hunter did take my car one week to have it worked on."

"Aha. That had to be it," Charlotte said.

We needed to talk with Hunter.

Once inside, I flipped the sign to OPEN. Wind Song jumped down and followed us across the room.

"Good job, Wind Song. Because of you we found stolen money in the car." I stroked her head, wishing I knew how she knew that.

She jumped up on the counter and looked in the direction of where I kept the treats.

"Yes, you definitely deserve a treat for that." I grabbed one from the bag and gave it to her.

I began my morning routine all the while trying to figure out how I would get the information from Hunter.

"You should have Ken help you," Charlotte piped up.

I hated to admit it. She was right, but Dylan wouldn't like me teaming up with Ken to solve the case. That seemed kind of like a betrayal.

The door opened and the UPS delivery man walked into the room. "I have a package for you."

I signed for it and set the box on the counter. I wasn't expecting anything.

"Is it a surprise?" Charlotte asked.

"It's from my mother. She hadn't mentioned anything." I grabbed the scissors and opened the box. "I guess we'll find out."

I took a black hat out of the box, then an envelope. I pulled the card from the envelope and read it. "The hat was my grandmother's. My mother just found it."

"It's beautiful."

Wind Song kept pawing at the box.

"What is it?" I moved the box so she couldn't reach it.

She jumped across the counter and knocked the box onto the floor.

"Look. Something else fell out." Juliana pointed to the floor.

I rushed around the corner of the counter and picked up a brooch.

"It's beautiful," Juliana said.

"I think it was on the hat," Charlotte said.

I placed the pin on the hat. "You're right."

Wind Song meowed and pawed at the hat. Then she touched my hand.

"I think she wants you to try it on," Charlotte said.

Everyone followed me over to the mirror and watched as I placed the hat on my head.

Juliana flashed her gorgeous smile. "It looks fabulous on you."

Wind Song meowed.

I realized then how much I looked like my grandmother when she was my age. No way I would offer this hat for sale. It would be part of my collection. Maybe someday I'd have a daughter to give it to. I hoped she'd love vintage as much as I did.

Chapter 28

Charlotte's Tips for a Fashionable Afterlife

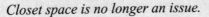

Closet space is no longer an issue.

Tonight, I was working extra late. I was in the back room of the shop, sorting through some items.

"Are you finished yet?" Charlotte said. "I'm all about hard work, but this is a little too much, Cookie."

"You're one to talk, Charlotte. You were a work-aholic."

"Yes, and look where that got me." She placed her hands on her hips.

"Well, a little hard work never hurt anyone. Plus, it's just me. I don't have help so I have to do this."

"Just don't work too much longer, okay?" she said.

"I promise," I said.

I finished hanging the items and then started out the door toward the front. When I heard a noise, I stopped in my tracks. I looked to the front and saw a man in my shop. He was wearing all black, even a mask, and looked like the man I'd seen at Regina's. Just like then, I could see only the back of him.

I didn't move. If he was a burglar, I didn't want to be shot. Along with Charlotte and Juliana, I was speechless. My mind raced. One wrong move and he would look over and see me. What was he looking for? I didn't have any cash in the place. Was he the same person who had broken in before? That person hadn't taken anything. Maybe this man wouldn't either. But why was he there?

Shaking with fear, I inched over to my right and hid behind a rack of clothing. I would just hang out there until he was gone. I didn't care what he took as long as he didn't hurt me. I peeked out and saw him grab a handful of the hats. Actually, he had all of them and took off for the door. I watched from between a bunch of dresses as he ran out the door.

I hoped it was safe for me to come out of hiding and hurried over to the front windows. When I peeked out, he was nowhere in sight.

"Cookie, you have to call the police right away," Charlotte said.

I pulled my cell phone from my pocket.

"What are you waiting on? Dial Dylan's number," she said.

"My phone is dead."

Charlotte groaned. "I told you that you should have a landline in the shop."

I shrugged. "No one has landlines anymore."

"They most certainly do and this is the prime

example of why you should." She put her hands on her hips.

"Okay, this is no time for arguing," Juliana said.

"I'll just have to call from someplace else."

"He might be out there waiting for you," Juliana said.

"I don't think he knew I was here." I opened the door and peeked out. Looking to my left and then to the right, I realized the sidewalks were empty. I inched out, fearful that he may actually be hiding just as Juliana had said.

"I want to know who that was." Charlotte whispered as if someone might actually hear her.

Both ghosts were tiptoeing behind me as if the burglar might actually see them. Now that I was outside, I wished that I was back inside. Actually, I wished that I was home, locked behind the door and safe.

"Apparently, the guy took off," Charlotte said.

"I guess so." I turned around to go back into the shop and saw someone walk quickly around the corner and into the alleyway. "Do you think that was him?" I whispered. "Did he come back for me?"

"I think he did." Worry was evident on Juliana's face.

"I'm not going to let him get away with this," Charlotte said.

The next thing I knew, she was stomping down the sidewalk.

"Charlotte," I whispered. "Don't go." Then I realized it was fine for her to go. She was a ghost. What could he do to her? It wasn't like he would even know she was there.

I had to find out what was going on and made my way over to the alleyway. Juliana followed me. Charlotte had made her way down the alley and was in front of the guy.

Somehow she managed to get the lid off the trash can and tossed it in front of him. He almost tripped to avoid it. Unfortunately, he got away with the armful of the hats. Fortunately, for me, I had come out of this with my life and wasn't hurt. Charlotte started walking back toward me, but within seconds she popped up beside me.

I jumped. "Don't do that. You scared me."

"You should be used to it by now," she said.

I glared at her. "I should be, but I'm not. So stop. How did you move the big trash can lid?"

"I'm just getting good with my ghostly skills." She wiggled her eyebrows.

"Do you think I should follow him down the alleyway?"

"At the speed he was running, you couldn't catch up with him. It's just pointless."

I blew the hair out of my eyes and stared down the alleyway anyway. I spotted one of my hats on the ground. "Hey, he dropped one."

At least he didn't get that one. I picked it up and brushed off the dirt. It made me sad to know that I had lost the hats. What would he do with them? Just toss them away when he realized they weren't the ones he was looking for.

"It had to be Victor, right?" I asked.

"You would think so," Charlotte said, "but this guy was taller."

"He was definitely taller than Victor," Juliana said.

I'd hoped her murder would be a quick case to solve. I was way wrong on that. The burglar was gone and I would never figure out who it was. We headed back to the shop.

"Are you going to report this?" Charlotte asked.

"You have to," Juliana said.

"I'll report it, but I don't think the police are going to be interested in finding hats for me. They have a murder case to solve. Plus, I don't know how many other things they have going on, so it won't be a priority for them."

"Don't be so negative. Maybe they will want to find the hats quickly. This has to be related to the murder," Charlotte said.

Once again the police would be at my shop. It was beginning to be a regular occurrence.

A couple minutes after I called Dylan he arrived with the sirens blaring and lights flashing. I opened the door, knowing he would ask if I was okay. It was beginning to be all he ever said to me. I was always getting myself into some kind of trouble.

"He took all my hats and ran down the alleyway. It can't be a coincidence that he wanted hats," I said, placing my hands on my hips. "I think this has something to do with the murder. I just have to fit the pieces of the puzzle together. Instead of telling me I shouldn't be involved maybe you should be asking me for help."

"But by being involved people are breaking into

your shop. You're in danger. I can't let that happen, Cookie."

"He cares for you, Cookie, but don't listen to him. We'll solve this murder," Charlotte said.

Maybe if I just got a good night's sleep I would be able to figure this out. Yeah, I'd already tried that.

The next morning I tried once again to keep things normal and had dressed in a 1950s winter white taffeta circle skirt that was so full I didn't even need a crinoline. My cardigan was winter white with rhinestone buttons down the front. My kitten heels were the same color.

I was in the shop going through my normal routine . . . although nothing seemed normal anymore. I had an empty display where the hats had been. I wasn't even going to bother to replace them until after the murder was solved and everything was over. Would it ever be over?

As I was moving the empty shelves, I noticed something on the ground.

"What's that?" Charlotte asked.

I reached down and picked up a set of keys. "Someone lost their keys. Could the burglar have lost his keys last night?"

"No way you'll find out," Charlotte said.

"Not so fast," I said. "Look at this."

"What is it?" she asked.

Juliana moved closer. "It's a library card attached to the key ring."

"What's that going to tell you?" Charlotte asked.

"I just so happen to have a friend who works for the library. She could possibly tell me who this card belongs to."

"Good thinking, Cookie. Great idea." Charlotte was in a generous mood all of a sudden.

"That's brilliant," Juliana said.

I picked up the phone—I'd charged it all night— to dial Carol Murray. We'd been friends since high school.

She answered on the first ring. "Cookie, what a pleasant surprise. How are you? I've been meaning to stop by your place."

"I didn't see you the last time I was at the library," I said.

"I took a vacation . . . to the beach."

I hated to move right from small talk into asking her for a favor, but I really needed it. After explaining the situation, she agreed to stop by on her way to work.

"I hope this works." Charlotte paced across the floor.

"It's certainly worth a shot," I said.

Fifteen minutes later, Carol walked through the door. She had a short bob hairstyle and big brown eyes. She wore a navy blue dress. I handed her the keys. I hated to remind her how important it was, but . . .

She took the keys. "I'll call you as soon as I find out anything, but don't tell anyone I'm doing this, okay?"

I shook my head. "I would never tell anyone."

Charlotte on the other hand would tell everyone. Luckily, she didn't have anyone to tell . . . other than me.

About an hour later Carol called. I dropped the necklace I was working on and answered the phone.

"I found a name for you," she said.

My heart sped up and my stomach fluttered with anticipation. Maybe it would be all for nothing. Maybe it was an old card or maybe a customer had lost her keys. Maybe the keys belonged to one of the men who'd been in the shop. I stopped those thoughts, remembering what Charlotte always reminded me. I had to keep a positive outlook and maybe positive things would come my way.

"Thank you for doing this," I said into the phone.

"The name on the card is Hunter Owens."

It was if the wind was knocked right out of me. "Are you serious?"

"I'm guessing you know this person?"

How would I tell Juliana? She would be very upset, but it wasn't something I would be able to keep from her. She and Charlotte were staring at me, waiting for the answer. As soon as I hung up they would want to know.

"Yes, I know him," I said, avoiding eye contact with them. "Thanks again." I immediately hung up the phone and dialed Dylan.

"Well, who was it?" Charlotte asked as I waited for him to pick up. "I can tell by the look on your face it's not good."

"She doesn't want me to know." Juliana stared at me. "Was it Hunter?"

I met her stare. "Yes, it was him." I hated to see the look of disappointment on her face. "I'm sorry."

"I'm sure there's a reasonable explanation," she said.

For her sake I hoped she was right.

I called Dylan and explained what I'd found. I just didn't tell him how I'd found out whose keys they were. He wanted to know, but I told him that I couldn't reveal my source. He didn't press the issue, thank goodness. Well, at least not right away. He would probably ask later. It was something I'd have to deal with . . . much later.

"Unfortunately, we have no proof that Hunter did anything, Cookie," Dylan said.

Somehow I knew he would say that. But what more proof did we need? I couldn't get a confession out of anyone.

"Listen, will I see you at the fall festival tomorrow?" Dylan asked. "Maybe you'll have some free time?"

I didn't bother to tell him that yes I'd have free time. When it came to social events I always had free time. He should know that by now. But I wanted him to think that maybe I had other plans. My Grandmother Pearl had always said it was good to keep them guessing. I didn't know if that was good advice or not, but I gave it a shot.

"Good. I'll stop by and see you?" he asked.

"I can give you a good deal on a candy apple. That's the booth I'm working tomorrow."

He laughed. "I'd like that."

"We should just go pay a visit to Hunter right now," Charlotte said.

I said good-bye to Dylan and motioned toward Juliana.

Charlotte stepped closer to me and whispered, "We can't baby her forever."

I would have to ease my way into asking her about visiting Hunter. I just didn't want any more trouble . . . but it looked as if the trouble was going to find me. I needed to take a more subtle approach rather than be brazen like Charlotte. That worked for her, but I wasn't sure it would work for me.

Wind Song was purring beside me. I stroked her across her back and asked, "What do you think, Wind Song?"

I was really hoping she had some advice for me— maybe from the Ouija board or the tarot cards—but she just closed her eyes and continued to purr. I guess she had no advice. Or perhaps she'd already given her advice. I truly was going to end up the crazy cat lady.

Soon she jumped down and went over to her window. That was her final statement. She didn't want to talk.

What was next for me? The only other option was to have a confrontation with Hunter. How else would I find out anything? I could return his keys. I wondered what he'd say about that. What he would say about how they got in my place? I was sure he would come up with some lame excuse. Juliana should haunt him. Maybe that would teach him a lesson. Maybe that would cause a confession. I wouldn't do anything yet. I'd wait and give it some extra thought.

Chapter 29

Cookie's Savvy Tips for Vintage Shopping

❦

If wearing pre-loved items bothers you,
vintage might not be for you.
However, you can always display
the vintage clothing as art.

I loved this time of year. With temperatures in the sixties it was a perfect day for the fall festival. Both the spring and fall festivals featured booths filled with the wares of the local stores. I was on the festival committee and had hired a couple high school students to run my booth while I ran the candy apple booth. I wanted to be a part of the festival as much as possible. Heather had done the same thing when I asked her to help me.

I wore a Lily Pulitzer floral dress with green, pink, and white colors throughout. For comfort I had on pink flats as we walked along the festival streets in the historic section of town. Main Street and some that connected to it had been closed so people could walk up and down as they went from booth to booth. Banners featuring beautiful colored leaves decorated the streetlights. Excitement filled the air.

I waved at Blanche who was running the hot chocolate booth. Mr. McDermott tried to get us to buy cotton candy as we passed by.

By the time we arrived at the booth we had customers waiting. We served them quickly—regular apples covered with red candy coating, caramel covered apples with nuts, or chocolate covered apples with sprinkles. I'd insisted on those and one was definitely going home with me. The money we raised was going toward refinishing buildings in town.

Heather was busy with a customer while I put out more apples.

"I wished there was something I could do to help," Charlotte said. "Y'all are busier than a one-armed wallpaper hanger."

"Just being here to keep us company is enough, Charlotte," I said over my shoulder.

"I never know if she's being serious," Charlotte whispered to Juliana.

I looked right at her. "I can hear you, you know. Of course I'm being serious. Charlotte, you know I love you."

She waved her hand dismissively, but I knew she loved me too.

When it had slowed down just a bit, I looked out over the crowd, happy to see all the residents having fun. It made up for some of the past events when such bad things had happened in Sugar Creek.

"Look who I see," Charlotte said, pointing across the way.

I followed her finger and spotted Ken.

"Isn't that adorable," Juliana said.

Ken was painting designs on children's faces. I had to admit seeing him made my heart go pitty-pat. I looked to my left and spotted Dylan. He was working security for the festival. He caught me watching and waved. I knew he would be over later to say hello. It was time for me to focus on selling more yummy apples. A line had formed quickly after just a short few minutes.

"You should add extra sprinkles," Charlotte said.

"Extra sprinkles are always a good idea," Juliana said.

I couldn't disagree. As far as sprinkles were concerned, more was better.

When things had slowed down again, Heather said, "Is it okay if I take a quick break?"

"Sure, I've got it from here." I picked up an apple—chocolate covered with sprinkles—and bit into it.

While waiting for another customer to approach, I listened to Charlotte and Juliana discuss the afterlife. When I turned around to straighten up the apples, someone cleared their throat from behind me. Charlotte and Juliana gasped. Victor was standing in front of me, flashing an evil smile.

"What is he doing here?" Charlotte said.

"It is really hard for me to be nice and help you," I said to him.

"I'd like a caramel apple with nuts," he said with that same evil smile.

"I'd like to give him a caramel apple," Charlotte said with a pump of her fist. She had been particularly feisty lately.

I handed him the apple and he handed me a few crumpled dollars.

"Thanks." He didn't take his eyes off me. "Seen any hats lately? Just be careful if you do. I wouldn't want you to get hurt."

"What is that supposed to mean?" Charlotte said.

That was what I wanted to know.

He took a bite of the apple then turned and walked away before I could ask.

"Was that a veiled threat?" I said.

"It most certainly seemed that way," Charlotte said.

"You should report him to the police," Juliana said. "And tell them what he asked."

"He'd said that I might get hurt. That could mean anything." Honestly, I felt like he was directing a threat toward me. As if I didn't have enough to worry about before. I would have to be more cautious but didn't know how I would exactly achieve that.

I spotted Heather walking back toward the booth. I wasn't going to tell her what happened. No reason for her to worry any more than she was already worrying. I would keep it all to myself and figure out a way to deal with it. Charlotte and Juliana didn't like that option, but I felt it was necessary.

* * *

After a full day of apples, caramel, and nuts it was time to go home. Not all of the nuts were on the apples either. Heather and I closed up the booth, finally ready to head home. Heather had parked behind the old movie theater and I had parked at the church. We were headed in different directions.

"See you in the morning." I tossed my hand up.

She waved and then took a bite out of her candy apple as she walked away.

"Your friend is really nice," Juliana said.

I agreed. "She's a special person. Not too many people like her in this world."

Dylan had told me to wait for him and he would walk me to my car, but he was so busy and wouldn't be finished for at least another thirty minutes. My feet were killing me so I decided to walk by myself. I made a shortcut through the alley and headed to the church parking lot. Plenty of people were still around so I didn't feel it was totally unsafe . . . until I heard someone walking behind me. That didn't necessarily mean anything bad, but it put me a little on edge. I turned around, but in the dark, I couldn't make out who it was.

The person didn't look particularly tall. Coming to a doorway on the side of the building, I decided to duck in and try to hide. I wanted to get a good look at who was following me. Well, if they were really following me. I stood in the doorway and waited. Footsteps echoed as they continued down the alley-way toward me. My anticipation increased with every step.

Once she stepped under the streetlight, I realized who had been following me.

"Aunt Regina. What is she doing here?" Juliana asked.

"Yes, I wonder," Charlotte said sarcastically.

"There's only one way for me to find out." As she passed the doorway, I stepped out.

She jumped back and screamed, clutching her chest. She looked at me with wide eyes. "Don't ever scare an old lady like that."

"She's not that old," Charlotte said.

"Just ask her what she's doing," Juliana said.

"Regina, are you lost?"

"She knows how to get out of here." Charlotte was being confrontational.

"I was just walking home from the festival," Regina said.

"That's a long way," Charlotte said.

"Were you following me?" I asked, looking her straight in the eyes.

She looked right back. "Why would I do something like that?"

"I suppose you wouldn't," I said, still suspicious.

"You scared me." She stared at me for a moment without answering.

"And you scared me." I looked up and noticed the hat on her head. It was one that I'd had in the store. One that had been stolen by Hunter. Why was she wearing it? "Where did you get that hat?"

She touched the hat. "Where did I get it?"

"Yes, that's what I asked."

"Um . . . I found it."

"She doesn't seem sure about that," Charlotte said.

"I'll give her the benefit of the doubt," Juliana said, but I knew even she was suspicious.

I continued questioning Regina. "Where did you find it?"

She waved her hand. "Just on the street."

"You don't just find hats on the street," Charlotte said.

"Sometimes you do," Juliana said.

"Well not hats like that," Charlotte said. "Unless you have a time machine."

Obviously, Regina wasn't going to tell me where she really found the hat. And I couldn't prove that it was mine, although I knew it was.

"Someone stole hats from my shop."

Regina narrowed her eyes. "Are you insinuating that I stole this hat?"

I had to defend my words. "Of course not. I just thought maybe the person who stole them had dropped it and you found it."

"Yes, that's probably what happened," she said.

"You just gave her an alibi," Charlotte said.

She would have come up with that one on her own anyway. But I wondered if it really was the truth. It was a reasonable thought. It made more sense than Aunt Regina *stealing* the hat. Or was she involved in the scheme to get the hat all along?

"Well, I must be going now." Regina walked around me and headed toward the end of the alley.

"Something stinks around here and it's not that trash can," Charlotte said.

Maybe Juliana didn't want to admit it, but I had to agree with Charlotte. Something smelled bad. I had to keep my eyes on Regina even more. I had to find out what was going on. I headed toward the end of alley. I hoped she wasn't waiting for me around the corner.

As I neared the end of the alleyway, someone grasped my shoulder. I screamed and punched with my elbow. The man let out a groan. When I turned around, Ken was behind me. Charlotte and Juliana really needed to pay more attention and alert me when someone was back there.

"Are you okay?" I asked, reaching out and grabbing his arm.

He waved it off. "You've got a nice elbow. I'm fine."

"I'm really sorry about that."

"I saw you walk down here and I was a little concerned."

"Did you see Regina?" I said.

Ken shook his head. "No. Where is she?"

"She was just here. I think she followed me, and get this. She had on one of the hats that were stolen from my shop."

"Really? How do you think she got it?" Ken asked.

I shrugged. "Your guess is as good as mine."

"It's possible that she found it."

"That was her excuse. I didn't want to accuse her of anything."

"Of course not," Ken said. "Can I walk you to your car?"

Happy that he offered, I grinned. "Who's going to walk you back?"

He smiled right back. "I'll take my chances."

We turned and walked down the rest of the alley. Just as I was ready to turn left toward the church parking lot I glanced back. Someone else stood at the other side of the alley and I was almost certain it was Dylan. Why hadn't he called me? I was sure he saw me walking with Ken, then he disappeared around the corner.

With Ken walking beside me, I continued on down the back sidewalk toward the parking lot.

Ken looked around, but didn't see anyone in the parking lot. "Where did she say she was going?"

"She said she was walking home." I opened my car door and slipped inside. "Maybe you should check on her."

He leaned on the open door. "I was just getting ready to say the same thing. Call me and let me know everything's okay."

"I'll let you know."

He closed the door and waved as he walked down the sidewalk.

"Dylan won't like that you were walking with Ken," Charlotte said.

I pulled out of the parking lot. "Don't remind me."

As I turned onto the next street, I spotted Regina having a deep conversation with someone.

"Maybe she needs a ride home," Juliana said.

When I saw who she was talking to I decided maybe she didn't need a ride. She was standing with Victor.

"I didn't think she knew him," Juliana said.

"I think that goes for all of us," I said.

I thought about pulling over and asking what they were talking about, but that would seem a little strange. Plus, they ended up getting into Victor's car.

"She must know him well enough to get in the car with him," Charlotte said.

"I don't like this," Juliana said. "He may have lured her into the car."

"That's possible," I said. "I should call Dylan and give him a heads-up."

"Maybe you should follow the car," Juliana said.

I made the next right so that I could turn around and fall in behind Victor's car. I just couldn't figure out why they would be talking. Were they discussing hats? Unfortunately, I couldn't find the car.

I might never know what they were talking about.

Chapter 30

Charlotte's Tips for a Fashionable Afterlife

❧

*You never have to worry if something fits
or go on a diet to fit into that little black dress.*

I'd just stepped into It's Vintage Y'all on Monday morning when my cell phone rang. I had several garments draped over one arm and in the other hand I held Wind Song's carrier.

I placed the carrier down, set the clothing on the counter, and grabbed the phone.

"Cookie, did I catch you at a bad time?" Ken asked when I answered.

"Of course not." I looked at the pile of clothing. Maybe I'd bought a little too much at yesterday's estate sale.

"Did you really need to buy those Jordache jeans?" Charlotte peered at the pile with disdain.

Okay. In my stressed out state, I'd made one bad decision. Occasionally it happened.

Focusing on the phone conversation, I asked, "Is everything okay?"

"I have good news for you. Well, I guess it's considered good news," he said.

"Okay, now I'm intrigued. What is it?" I opened the carrier door and Wind Song sashayed out.

"I found someone who may have witnessed something with Juliana's murder."

"Did you tell the police?" I asked.

"I left a message, but they didn't seem interested."

"That seems odd. Who did you tell? Was it Dylan?" I pressed.

"No, it was another detective."

Of course. I should have known that he wouldn't call Dylan.

"Anyway, I thought you might want to talk with this person. I would go, but I can't get out of court until later today."

I grabbed a notepad and pen. "I understand. I'm glad you called." I preferred that I talked with the person anyway, though it was sweet of him to offer. "What's the name?"

"Her name is Renee and she works at the Primo Café."

I scribbled down the info. "So it's the café not far from where Juliana was found?"

"Yes, that's the place."

I was supposed to meet Juliana there that morning. Since then, driving that road always brought back the memory. Wondering if I could find a different route, I thanked Ken for the info.

"Are you sure he couldn't come with us?" Charlotte asked.

I punched the OFF button on the phone. "Positive."

Charlotte and Juliana waited all afternoon for time to close the shop so that we could go to the café. I was nervous. Not just because we had to go in the direction of Juliana's murder, but because I wasn't sure what the supposed witness would say. I wasn't even sure if she would be there.

I closed up and they followed me out to the car. Wind Song was in her carrier, though she'd acted restless and hadn't wanted to go in.

After dropping off Wind Song at home, I pointed the car in the direction of the café.

"Oh, are we going on that street?" Charlotte asked.

"Well, I had thought about going a different way, but I thought maybe seeing the surroundings again would trigger a memory."

"It will trigger a memory all right, but I doubt it will be a good one."

Juliana spoke up. "You know I'm sitting right back here and can hear everything y'all say, right? Your whispering doesn't really work."

"Sorry, Juliana. We were just trying to keep from upsetting you."

She flashed her sad-eyed look at me. "It's okay. I'm used to being upset."

"That's so sad," Charlotte said.

"Don't be upset, Juliana," I said. "I'll figure this out. I promise."

She forced a smile. "If anyone can, I know you will, Cookie."

I tapped my fingers against the steering wheel, feeling more pressure to solve this case than ever. Juliana was counting on me. After all, I owed it to her. Maybe if she hadn't been driving to meet me, she wouldn't have been shot. I knew she would deny anything like that, but I felt guilty nonetheless.

As we approached the scene of the crime, I wasn't sure if I should speed past or slow down. Finally, I decided to just drive a normal speed.

"Does anything come back to you?" Charlotte asked.

Juliana stared out the window. "No, nothing at all. I just remember driving and the next thing I knew I was talking with Cookie."

I drove past and soon came to the café. I pulled in the parking lot and found a spot. "Fingers crossed that this goes well," I said as I opened the car door.

Charlotte and Juliana got out too. I would probably feel less nervous if they'd stayed in the car. I knew that wasn't happening though.

I entered the café. It was six o'clock so the dinner crowd was growing quickly. I looked around and spotted a woman watching me.

She immediately walked over. "You look a little lost. You can sit wherever you like . . . if you can find a spot."

"Do you work here?" I asked.

"No, my sister does. Everyone is busy. I thought

I'd let you know so you wouldn't stand here for a long time."

"Thanks." I spotted an empty table by the window and headed over.

"This place is quaint," Charlotte said as she looked around. Not many places got her approval.

After waiting a couple more minutes the woman came back over. "I thought I'd help out again. My sister will be over in a second to take your order. In the meantime, can I get you something to drink?"

"It looks as if they need to hire more staff," Charlotte said.

I hadn't expected to eat, but I supposed it would look strange if I didn't. "I'd like water with lemon please."

"Be right back," she said.

"I wonder which one she is," Juliana asked.

"I can barely tell customer from staff," Charlotte said.

The woman came back over with my water. "You've never been here before?"

I shook my head. "No, this is the first time. Actually, I came here to speak with Renee."

"Oh, that's my sister. I'm Gale. Can I help you with something?" She kept her eyes on me.

"Well, I wanted to talk with her about the murder." I hated to just blurt it out, but I didn't know what else to do.

Just then a dark-haired woman approached with an apology and a smile. "Sorry it took me so long. What can I get you?"

Maybe she wouldn't be so friendly when she figured out what I wanted.

"I was told you might have some information about the murder."

Renee exchanged a look with her sister.

"I'll let you two talk." Gale walked away.

Renee looked at me again. "What do you want to know?"

"Have you spoken with the police yet?"

"Actually, no. See, I didn't realize that I had been witness to anything until the other day. When I read the story about what happened, it sparked a memory. My boyfriend knows Ken, so he told him about it. I wasn't comfortable going to the police. I wasn't sure that I wanted to get involved. Ken said you would be stopping by to talk with me. I'm glad he didn't tell the police."

I didn't have the heart to tell her that he had left them a message, but it looked as if they weren't taking him seriously.

"So what did you see?" I asked.

"I was walking out to my car when I saw a man come out of the bushes. He looked around and acted kind of strange."

"This is huge," Charlotte said, getting closer.

"Could you pick him out if you saw him?" I asked.

She shook her head. "Unfortunately, I couldn't. He was wearing a mask."

"Didn't you think that was kind of odd?"

She shrugged. "Well, it's almost Halloween, so I really didn't think anything of it."

"Hasn't this woman ever seen a scary movie? Did she see the Michael Myers character in *Halloween*?" Charlotte said.

"Can you tell me what kind of mask he was wearing?" That info would be better than nothing. "Perhaps what clothing he was wearing?"

"All black. You know, like someone trying to conceal their appearance with the cover of night. Except it wasn't night. I'm not sure about the mask. It was just something creepy."

"Thanks." *It had taken her awhile to remember that tiny bit, so maybe she would think of something else important.* I handed her my card. "Can you call me if you think of anything else?"

She read the card and then said, "Sure, I'll give you a call."

I was too upset by the smidgen of information, so I decided not to eat.

Chapter 31

Cookie's Savvy Tips for Vintage Shopping

❧

**Learn the difference between
vintage and thrift stores.**

In the mail about a month ago, I'd received an invitation to the historic society's charity event. With all that had been going on lately, the event had almost slipped my mind completely. The fact that I was going alone was a big disappointment for Charlotte.

"I told you, Charlotte. Dylan has to work. I decided not to ask him or anyone."

She placed her hands on her hips. "Maybe he could've gotten off work if you had given him notice."

I pulled the gown out of the closet. "There was no need for him to even try. It's not that big a deal."

"Well, then you could've asked Ken. I'm sure he would've loved to have gone with you. How handsome he would look in a tuxedo."

I took the dress off the hanger. "I can't ask him. Besides, there's nothing wrong with going alone."

She studied her fingernails. "If you say so."

My red gown had a full bias cut skirt with pleats at the waist. The shoulder straps criss-crossed in the back. A sash rested at the waist and looped around to a swag at the back bodice. I slipped into the red gown and zipped up the back.

After putting on heels, I asked Charlotte, "How do I look?"

"Stunning. Very Ginger Rogers. That's why you shouldn't waste all of this going alone." She pointed to my face. "A little more blush would be nice."

"Thank you for the compliment, but can we just let this go?" I swiped the makeup brush across my cheeks.

Juliana looped her arm around Charlotte. "Come on, Charlotte. We'll enjoy the evening. She doesn't need a date."

"Thank you, Juliana."

Charlotte looked from her to me. "I suppose it will be nice to get out for a lovely evening for a change. Just remember this is a special event. I've been many times. I'm glad to finally get back."

I finished my outfit with diamond earrings and a matching necklace and bracelet set. I grabbed a black clutch that matched my shoes.

"This is so sad, Cookie. Did you go to prom alone?" Charlotte asked.

I walked out the door, not even noticing the dark clouds overhead. "No, Charlotte, I did not go alone. Maybe my date was bad, but I wasn't alone."

"Nothing wrong with going alone to the prom," Juliana said.

"Thank you again, Juliana." At least she was sticking up for me. "Now can we drop this? We're on our way. Let's have a good evening."

It was only a short drive, but Charlotte had finally gotten off the subject.

I pulled up to the community center where the event was being held. "Wow, this is nice. They have valet parking this evening," I said as we pulled up to the front door.

"I told you it was a special event," Charlotte said.

We got out of the car and I walked into the event. "I've never seen this many people in this building at one time."

Everyone looked great—men in their tuxedos and women in their evening gowns.

"Cookie, you're the absolute most beautiful woman here."

"Why, thank you, Charlotte. That was very kind of you." I knew by the compliment that she was up to something.

"Oh, look who's here." Charlotte pointed across the room.

I watched her pointing finger, spotted Ken, and asked, "Did you know he was going to be here?"

She made a funny sound. "How could I possibly know? I'm not psychic. And so what if I did? It doesn't mean anything."

Just then he looked at me and headed across the room toward me. He didn't take his eyes off me, smiling all the way.

Charlotte whistled. "I knew it. He looks fantastic in that tuxedo."

She was right. He did look wonderful.

"Cookie, I'm glad you came tonight. You look stunning."

"Thank you. You look great too," I said.

"Would you care to dance?" he asked.

"Say yes. Say yes," Charlotte said.

"You should definitely say yes," Juliana said.

"Yes, I'd love to." Smiling was unavoidable. After all, it was just one dance. No harm in that, right?

He took my hand, led me to the dance floor, and held me in his arms. His woodsy scent encircled me in a hug. Charlotte and Juliana stayed on the sideline, watching. When I glanced over, they waved. I was surprised they hadn't wanted to dance around us so they could hear the conversation.

With my arms wrapped around his waist, I said, "I didn't know you were coming tonight."

"The president of the society invited me. I thought about not coming. Now I'm glad I did." He stared straight into my eyes.

With romantic music filling the air, it was way too intimate. I panicked and said, "I'll be right back."

Before Ken could respond, I turned and hurried away. In a matter of seconds, Charlotte and Juliana were beside me.

"What happened? Why did you stop dancing with him?" Charlotte demanded from over my shoulder.

"I don't know what I'm thinking." I waved my hand.

"Where are you going now?" Charlotte asked. "Don't tell me you're leaving."

"I'm not leaving. I'm just going to the ladies' room to freshen up my lip gloss." I smiled, trying to hide my uneasiness. "After that I'll get back out there and dance with him."

Charlotte held her hands up. "Don't get your knickers in a bunch."

As I neared the restroom, footsteps sounded from behind me. When I glanced back, no one was there.

"That was strange. Did you hear that?" I whispered.

Charlotte and Juliana nodded their answers in silence.

"Someone was back there." Charlotte peered down the long hallway.

"Did you see them?" I asked.

"No," Charlotte said. "But I heard it."

I was a little spooked. Walking into the ladies' room, I stood in front of the mirror. I had to get my thoughts together. As I applied the lip gloss across my lips, the footsteps returned. The echoing sound was distinct and it was right outside the door.

I paused with the makeup in my hand. "I thought for sure someone was right outside the door. Are they coming in?"

The footsteps sounded again, as if the person was walking away.

Charlotte poked her head out. "No one's out there."

Just then smoke seeped in from the nearby vent.

Panic took hold immediately. "What's happening?" Fear danced in my stomach.

"Cookie, there's a fire. You have to get out of here right away." Charlotte motioned for me to hurry.

Smoke was coming in stronger. "This can't be happening."

"There's no way you can stand this for very long," Charlotte said. "Get out of here now."

I ran over to the door and pulled on the knob, but nothing happened. "The door's stuck."

"Oh, it can't be. Try again." Charlotte pounded on the door, but her hands went right through.

As hard as I could, I pulled on the door again. It didn't budge. The fact that the smoke was still coming in made my anxiety surge. A full-fledged panic attack had set in as I yanked on the door. Not surprisingly, still nothing happened. With one more pull I tumbled backwards, almost falling. I stumbled in the heels, but managed to right myself.

"I can't believe this is happening," Juliana said.

The realization of being trapped finally hit me. I pounded on the door, but nothing happened.

"Okay, take a deep breath and just calm down. Banging on the door isn't going to help," Charlotte said.

"Of course it will help," I said. "Maybe someone will hear me and get me out of here. Plus, I can't take a deep breath. I'll inhale the smoke. That's a clear way to get me to check out faster. Do you want me dead?"

She glared at me. "Of course I don't want you dead. How dare you say that."

"I'm not bickering with you right now." I waved off her comment and moved across the room. I took off running toward the door, slammed right into it, and fell backwards on my butt. Stunned a bit, I groaned as I managed to climb up from the floor.

"What in the Sam Hill are you doing?" Charlotte asked.

"I'm trying to break the door down." I rubbed my shoulder.

"That's never going to happen. You weigh like one hundred pounds."

"I weigh more than one twenty, but whatever."

"You're like the size of a squirrel."

Trying to break the door had been a bad idea. I was freaking out and not making the best decisions at the moment.

"You have a phone, right?" Juliana said. "Call Dylan."

"Why didn't I think of that?"

"You're not good under pressure," Charlotte said. "Tell him you need to be saved."

I grabbed my bag from the counter and pulled out the phone. As soon as Dylan answered, I said in a panic, "I'm stuck in the bathroom and there's a fire."

"Where are you?" he asked, clearly freaking out.

"I'm at the Sugar Creek Community Center for the historic society charity event." I rushed my words.

"I'm on my way. Can you get out?"

If I could escape the inferno I wouldn't have called him . . . but whatever. "No. It's stuck."

"I'm on my way." He ended the call.

With my phone still in my hand, it rang. Ken's number was displayed on the screen.

"Cookie, where are you?" he asked in a panic when I picked up the phone. "There's a fire in the building. Everyone's outside, but I can't find you."

Maybe I should've told him where I was going

and I wouldn't be stuck with the fire all around me. What were the odds? Just my luck to be trapped in the bathroom during a fire.

"I'm in the restroom and I can't get out. The door is stuck. I'm—" The phone went dead.

Smoke was filling up the small space and I was finding it harder to breathe.

"Get down on the floor." Charlotte dropped to the floor.

I knew that was what I was supposed to do, but somehow it felt as if once I was on the floor I would never get up again. As long as I stayed upright, I might be able to fight. Fighting fire was impossible for me alone. I had the ghosts, but they couldn't help.

"Don't worry, Cookie. It'll be all right." Charlotte tried to calm me, but her voice was full of panic.

"They'll find you in time. Just stay calm," Juliana said.

I needed the encouraging words from them.

"I'll be right back," Charlotte said.

"No, don't leave me here." I reached for her, but she'd popped out the door. "Juliana, don't you leave right now." They were all that I had.

Charlotte popped back through the door. "They're on their way. It's Ken and Dylan."

It was a good feeling to know that the police were on their way. I coughed and tried to stay alert. If I passed out, it would all be over. I had an uncomfortable thought. If Dylan saw Ken in his tux and me in the gown he'd think that we came together. I closed my eyes. I couldn't worry about that. I needed out of this room. That was most important.

"Cookie, stand back from the door," Dylan yelled.

I ran to the back of the room, coughing. The next thing I knew, Dylan had busted the door down. Through the smoke, he and Ken emerged at the door at the same time, as if they were in a race to see who could reach me first. Ken grabbed one arm, Dylan the other, and they guided me toward the hallway. Smoke filled the hall, but at least it was less intense.

"Don't worry, Cookie. We're almost out." Even in spirit form, Charlotte took on the appearance that only a high stress situation would bring.

Thank goodness we reached the outside of the building. That was a close one. My life had flashed before my eyes. Fire trucks with lights flashing surrounded the building. Water hoses were out and people were standing around watching. The paramedics raced over to us and guided me to the back of an ambulance.

"You don't need to do this." I waved off the young brown-haired technician.

"Cookie, you need to let them check you out," Ken said.

Dylan looked over at Ken. "We got it from here. Thanks for your help."

The look on Ken's face made me extremely sad. I was grateful that both of them had risked their lives to help me. "I think both of you need to be checked out too. You were in there as well. No arguing."

"Cookie, I don't have time. I'm fine. Trust me," Dylan said.

A police officer motioned to Dylan. He looked as

if he didn't want to leave me alone with Ken. He knew Ken wasn't going anywhere until it was all over. Finally he said, "I'll be right back." Dylan gave one last look at Ken and then walked away.

"Are you sure you're okay?" Ken asked me. He'd refused to be seen by a paramedic.

"I'm fine. Did you hear what happened? What caused it?"

Ken looked back at the building. "The fire chief thinks it might be lightning. It was storming pretty bad."

"Yeah, but at least it looks like they got the fire out."

Smoke still came from the top, but the structure looked as if it wasn't damaged too badly.

"You're just lucky they saved you," Charlotte said.

She didn't have to remind me.

Someone called Ken over.

"I'll be right back, okay?" he said to me.

"I'll be here." I anticipated staying there. Honest. The paramedics said I was fine, but I figured I needed the rest.

When I noticed Victor across the way, staying put wasn't an option. It seemed extremely odd that he would be there. Sure, people were watching the scene, but I was suspicious of him.

Juliana noticed me staring. "You see him too?"

"You have to find out why he's here," Charlotte said.

He turned and started to walk away.

It couldn't hurt for me to follow him, just for a bit

to see where he went. Peering around, I realized that no one was paying attention to me. I eased away from the ambulance and weaved around a crowd of people. I kept my eyes on him so I wouldn't lose him.

Victor slipped around the side of the fire engine and made his way across the grassy area that led to the back of the building.

I was afraid the police had blocked off the whole area, but so far it remained open for anyone to access. I tried to stay back a ways so he wouldn't catch me following him. He moved around a big oak tree and then around the side of the building. I'd made good progress until my heel got stuck in the grass and I fell forward into the mud.

"Oh, Cookie. Look at you now," Charlotte said. "You look like you're fighting a pig in slop."

Charlotte always knew how to make me feel better at the worst moments.

I was trying to get up when all of a sudden someone grabbed my arm from behind. I drew my arm back and made contact with that person's face.

Ken groaned and held his cheek.

"Oh my! Ken, are you okay?" I asked.

"Oh, Cookie. What have you done now? This just goes from bad to worse." Charlotte clutched her chest.

"I'm fine. A little rattled, maybe." Ken wiped his hands on his pants.

"Cookie, you hit like a girl." Charlotte placed her hand over her eyes as if she couldn't bear the sight.

I am a girl so that *kind of* made sense.

"What are you doing over here?" Ken asked.

"I saw Victor and thought it was odd for him to be here. He walked around back."

"You've been through a lot of stress. Let's go back up front," Ken said, helping me across the wet grass.

Did he think I had imagined it? Maybe he was right. I had been through a traumatic experience tonight. It could have been someone who looked like Victor.

Chapter 32

Charlotte's Tips for a Fashionable Afterlife

*With no hassles, you can change
your lipstick color or nail polish
as often as you want.*

The next morning, I was sorting through a pile of
old costume jewelry when the door caught my attention. My nerves set in as soon as I spotted who it was.
Victor had returned. He was looking for the specific
hat, but I couldn't prove that yet.

He spotted me watching him and walked in my
direction. I knew I would not be able to get away from
his confrontation.

"What are you going to say to him, Cookie?"
Juliana asked.

"Tell him you're not going to put up with any nonsense out of him. You call Dylan and have him escort
Victor out of this place." Charlotte circled around him.

The ghosts were excited. I knew Charlotte meant business.

I moved around the counter and headed over to Victor. I'd tell him I had no hats and that was that. I just had to be stern. I pushed my shoulders back and held my head high. "May I help you find anything?"

He looked me up and down as if to say I should know what he was looking for. Of course I knew, but I was going to make him ask first.

"This guy is up to no good." Charlotte crossed her arms in front of her chest and tapped her foot against the floor.

"He gives me the creeps." Juliana rubbed her arms. "I should know him from somewhere, but my memory is blank."

That had happened when she made the transition to the afterlife.

Finally Victor looked at me and said, "Did you ever have a chance to go through those hats? Remember I asked you about a hat? You said you were going to call me."

"He seems confrontational," Charlotte said.

She was right. There was an edge to his voice that hadn't been there before. It seemed as if his patience was running thin with me locating the hat.

"Actually, I didn't find anything. I'm sorry I forgot to call you, " I said, making it seem like I was a bad business woman. This was a different circumstance. I doubted he would be back in for more vintage items anytime soon . . . hopefully never.

He reached in his pocket.

"Oh my gosh. He's got a gun." Charlotte hid behind the counter, Juliana following.

Yes, they were being slightly dramatic.

Victor pulled out a picture. "This is a picture of the hat I'm looking for."

I didn't need to see it to know what the hat would look like, but peered down at the photo anyway. Sure enough, it was the hat that Juliana had had in her car.

Charlotte and Juliana peeked up from behind the counter.

"Thank goodness he didn't kill her," Charlotte said.

I decided to question Victor a little. "Why are you interested in this specific hat?"

He looked at me suspiciously.

"He doesn't seem to like that question," Charlotte said.

"It was a good question, I thought," Juliana said.

I'd struck a nerve. Wind Song jumped down from the window and raced over to us. She peered up at Victor and hissed. He scowled at her and took a few steps away.

"Let him have it, Wind Song," Charlotte said.

"Are you just playing games with me?" Victor asked.

"Oh, this doesn't look like it's going to end well," Charlotte said. "I knew he was mean."

I tried to remain professional. "I'm sorry I don't have the hat you're looking for. I'm definitely not playing games."

He narrowed his eyes and moved a little closer to me. "The money was originally hidden under the brim inside the hat. I want to make sure I get all the money." Wind Song hissed again.

"I don't like where this is going, Cookie. We need to get away from this guy," Charlotte said.

I had the same thought, but I didn't know what to do. He took another step closer and my heart sped up. It looked as if he was ready to strangle me.

Wind Song hissed and then jumped in the air with her paws stretched out. She scratched at him. He held his arms up and managed to block most of her attempts, but she made contact on his face once.

I couldn't believe she was trying to protect me. She'd never done anything like that before.

The next thing I knew, Ken grabbed Victor and slammed him to the floor. Victor tossed a few colorful words at him. In almost one motion, Ken picked Victor up from the ground, escorted him to the door, opened it, shoved him out, and closed the door behind him . . . as if he'd just taken out the trash.

"Way to go, Ken," Charlotte said.

"That'll show him," Juliana said.

Wind Song climbed onto the counter, reached out, and licked my hand.

"Oh, Wind Song, are you all right?" I hugged her. "Thank you for saving me."

"Forget about the cat. Thank Ken," Charlotte said.

I turned to him. "Thank you for getting rid of that guy."

"Not a problem. It looked like he wasn't here for vintage clothing."

I straightened my hair and shirt. "In a sense, but

he was looking for a hat. I think he might be the murderer."

Ken's eyes widened. "Well, based on his behavior, it wouldn't be a shock. What kind of hat was he looking for and why?"

I explained the situation with the hat. "So the money was originally in the hat and that's why everyone wanted it."

"Are you calling the police?" Ken didn't even like mentioning Dylan's name. He knew that I would call Dylan and tell him what happened.

"This is a whole other macho side of Ken that I've never seen," Charlotte said, almost swooning.

Her affection swayed easily from one guy to the other, but it was easy to see why.

"I don't think he came in here only to save you, Cookie," Juliana said

"Ask him why he stopped by," Charlotte said.

Oh yeah. Suddenly, I was curious what had brought him by. "So you didn't come by to just save me from an unruly customer . . . or the potential murderer."

Ken chuckled. "No, actually that wasn't the only reason." He pulled a piece of paper from his pocket. "I found this notice for an estate sale and thought you'd want to know about it."

"Isn't that just the sweetest thing? He's always thinking of you, Cookie." Charlotte liked to think of things as a fairytale sometimes.

I doubted that bringing by the notice meant he was thinking of me *all the time*. "I appreciate that. Thank you." I took the paper from him.

He stared at me for a moment and then said, "So you'll call me if you need help? I'm worried about you."

I waved my hand. "I'll be fine. Thank you."

He accepted my assurance with a smile and then walked out the door.

I immediately picked up the phone and dialed Dylan. He would probably come over right away.

"You have to file a police report," Charlotte said.

"I'm on it," I said.

Unfortunately, Dylan didn't answer my call, and I was forced to leave a message.

When I hung up, Charlotte said, "That sounded like a rambling mess."

"Well, I feel like rambling mess. I hope Victor doesn't return, but I have a feeling he will be back."

"You need to be ready for him the next time he shows up," Charlotte said.

"Any ideas on what I should do?" I asked.

"You'll think of something," Juliana said.

"Thanks for the help. Both of you."

We stared at the window for moment, wondering if he would return.

Chapter 33

Cookie's Savvy Tips for Vintage Shopping

❦

*Proper storage is key to any
vintage garment. Store them in a dry place
and avoid plastic storage.*

The ghosts and I were headed through town in my
Buick. The comfort of my bed was calling to me.
After a long bath I planned on curling up with a good
book. While waiting at the red light at the corner of
Rowan and Fourth Street, I happened to glance to my
left to see the burned community center building.
That brought back chilling memories.

"That's the car. That's Victor's car," Juliana said
suddenly.

She was right. The maroon Kia sedan was parked in
the middle of the lot, but Victor was nowhere in sight.
I was grateful for that. Although I wanted to solve the
crime, I didn't want to have another confrontation
with Victor. That didn't mean I wouldn't do it though.

"You have to go over there and check it out," Charlotte said.

"I'm not sure what good it will do to look, but I'll give it a shot." I tapped my fingers against the steering wheel.

The light turned green and I pushed the gas. Unfortunately, I couldn't switch lanes fast enough to make the turn.

"Go up and around the block." Charlotte pointed forward.

I hoped that he didn't leave before I got back around. What if he saw me snooping around? My shiny red Buick stood out like a neon sign. I made the next left and then down to the light.

"Cut through the back alley and work your way over to the parking lot." Charlotte ordered.

Wind Song was meowing in her carrier. She clawed at the door.

"I think she wants out," Juliana said.

"I'm not sure that's a good idea." I made the next left into the parking lot and stopped a few spaces from Victor's car.

"Oh, she just wants to see what's going on. What harm can it do?" Charlotte said.

I turned off the ignition. "I guess I can let her out as long as she promises not to run out of the car when I open the door."

Wind Song meowed in agreement to my offer.

After getting out of the car, I climbed into the backseat and let Wind Song out of the carrier. She stretched and then climbed up to look out the back window.

"Good, kitty." I closed the door so she couldn't escape.

Charlotte and Juliana followed me out of the car. The place was empty of people. There weren't many cars either. Someone could be watching us though. Well, watching me since they couldn't see the ghosts.

As I moved closer to his car, my heart rate sped up. What if he jumped out and grabbed me? I released a deep breath, trying to calm down. Unless he was hunkered down by the side of the car, it didn't look as if there was anywhere else he could hide.

"What exactly are we looking for?" I asked.

The ghosts were quiet.

"Y'all don't exactly know either."

Charlotte waved her hand. "You might get lucky and find something you didn't know you were even looking for."

I felt a headache coming on after that statement. With nerves dancing in my stomach, I leaned down and peered into the car. Junk food wrappers and used cups littered the seats and floor.

"Do you see anything?" Charlotte asked.

"I see one thing." The sight of the object sent a shiver down my spine. "There's a gun on the car seat. Right there." I tapped the window.

"Are the doors unlocked?" Juliana asked.

I grabbed the handle and pulled the door open. "I can't believe he left it unlocked with the gun right there."

"He also steals from people, so I don't think he's the sharpest knife in the drawer."

"Good point, Charlotte," I said.

Since I wasn't trained with firearms, I decided it was best that I didn't touch the gun. However, I poked around the rest of the car. As I suspected, I found nothing. "I should call Dylan and let him know about the car and the gun."

Maybe it was the murder weapon they'd been looking for. That would be enough to arrest Victor and bring justice for Juliana.

"What do you think you're doing?" a male voice asked.

Charlotte and Juliana screamed with me. Fear raced through me. Victor was quickly approaching us. An angry snarl curled his lips.

"What do we do now?" Charlotte said.

"I have no clue." I scrambled back, hitting my head on the top edge of the car.

Victor saw me talking to myself, but that was the least of my worries at the moment. The look on his face let me know he was ready to let me have it. Getting away from him seemed impossible. He had me blocked.

"You have to think of something quick," Charlotte said.

"There's nothing to think of." My stomach clenched with one of my intuitions. "It's pretty obvious what I was doing."

"Are you stealing from me?" His eyes were ruthless and remote.

"No, of course not."

"It sure looks like you were. You better explain yourself before I snap you in two." He made a breaking motion with his hands.

"That doesn't sound like it would be good, Cookie," Charlotte said.

"You're telling me," I said.

His dark eyebrows drew together in a scowl. "Who are you talking to?"

"I have ghosts standing beside me. You happen to know one of them. It's Juliana. Remember her? You killed her." I didn't take my eyes off him.

His eyes widened. "I didn't kill anyone." His gaze shifted to beside me. "Are you crazy? You think you're talking to ghosts?"

"He makes me so mad. I'd like to show him." Charlotte pumped her fist.

I wanted to move to my right, hoping that I could make it over to my car, but he was watching every move I made. "I know you killed Juliana."

His jaw tightened. "You need to keep quiet and stop messing around. You shouldn't have been in my car. Now I'm going to have to get rid of you."

"Oh, Cookie, this is bad. I don't know how you're going to get out of this situation." Juliana sounded as if she was almost in tears.

"She's a goner," Charlotte said.

"You're not helping, Charlotte. You're supposed to be motivating and reassuring."

"That's all I've got right now." She gestured toward Victor. "Look at him. He has rage in his eyes."

I held my head high. "We know you hid money in Juliana's car. We found it."

His face turned pale. "You found the money. Where was it?"

I smirked. "I thought you knew it was in her car."

"Do you have the money?" He grinned with a malevolence that turned my blood to ice water.

I crossed my arms in front of my chest. "Are you crazy? As if I would give it to you. The police have the money and you'll never get it now."

"Cookie, don't antagonize him," Charlotte said.

Victor moved a few steps closer to us. Another surge of panic coursed through my body. Out of the corner of my eye, I caught movement. Heather stood by my car. I didn't want him to see her. How had she gotten here? When I scanned the lot, I spotted her car. She must have noticed me there and stopped to see what I was doing.

He took a few more steps. The closer he came, the more evident the look of fury on his face became. The snarl appeared more sinister.

Heather noticed what was going on and inched a bit closer. She was up to something. She took a few more careful steps. Without saying a word, she reached down and took off her shoe. In one fluid motion, she pulled her arm back and tossed the leather clog at Victor's head. It was a good thing she had always been athletic. The less-than-fashionable shoe made contact with his head. He yelped and fell to the ground.

"Quick! Do something, Cookie," Charlotte yelled.

As far as I remembered, I'd never moved so quickly. I spun around and grabbed the gun from the car. My hands shook. What would I do with this thing? Of course it was better I had it than Victor.

With my trembling hands, I pointed the Glock at

him, realizing it was just like Dylan's. "Don't make a move." At least I had the upper hand now.

Surprisingly, Victor threw his hands in the air. "You won't shoot."

"Way to go, Cookie," Charlotte said.

"You got it, Cookie," Juliana said.

Heather raced over to us. "Cookie, are you all right?"

My hands still shook as I pointed the gun at Victor. "I've had better days. What about you?"

Victor remained silent. He was probably plotting how to get the gun from me.

She blew the hair out of her eyes. "Yeah, I was scared for a minute."

"Thanks for throwing the shoe. You gave me a chance to get his gun."

Her gaze darted from me to Victor. "I didn't know what else to do."

"You won't get away with this," Victor snapped. "Why don't you put the gun down? It's not loaded anyway."

No way would I fall for that trick. The criminal always told the person who had the gun that it wasn't loaded. I'd seen that in the movies.

"I'll take my chances," I said, still aiming the gun at him. "Heather, get my phone out of the car and call the police."

"Not so fast, ladies," a male voice said from the dark.

Chapter 34

Charlotte's Tips for a Fashionable Afterlife

❧

*Shoulder pads, leg warmers, fanny packs,
and bike shorts are just as hideous in the afterlife
as they were when you were alive.*

When we looked to the right, Hunter was standing not far away. He had a gun pointed at us. The intensity of his stare seared through me and I had to look away.

"Put the gun down, Cookie, or your friend gets it." His hand didn't shake like mine.

"Hunter, what are you doing?" Juliana's voice caught in her throat.

"Victor and I had a meeting," he said.

"How could you do this? You were involved in this? I love you . . ." The words faded to a whisper.

"Men are scum, Juliana," Charlotte said.

It was not the time for Charlotte's world viewpoint.

It looked as if I had no choice but to put the gun down. Making no sudden movements, I slowly placed the gun down on the ground.

"Now move away from the car." Hunter motioned with the gun.

What was he going to do to us?

"Victor get up, man," Hunter yelled.

"I can't believe they were in on this together. All along, I trusted him. I . . ." Juliana's words drifted off as she was lost in betrayal.

I heard the anguish in her voice. "Your girlfriend is here—her ghost. She's upset. She can't believe you did this to her."

Hunter looked at Victor.

Victor shrugged. "She's crazy."

Laughter rumbled deep in Hunter's chest. "So now you see ghosts? I thought that was what your crazy friend did for a living." He pointed at Heather. "She runs that kooky store in town, right? I didn't know you were that way too."

"Nobody makes fun of my friends." Charlotte stomped over and shoved him.

Of course it did nothing.

He frowned as if he felt the breeze her movements had caused.

"Tell him that I know he dressed up as a bunny rabbit when he was eight years old and everyone made fun of him," Juliana said.

I repeated what Juliana had said.

Instantly the smile slipped off his face. "How do you know that?"

"I told you her ghost is here. She's going to get revenge against you. No matter if you kill me, she'll still get back at you."

His frown turned to a glower. "I don't believe you."

"Suit yourself," I said.

"That's enough talking. Get away from the car. You're coming with us." Victor reached down, grabbed the gun, and pointed it at me while Hunter aimed at Heather.

Since Heather and I could pretty much do nothing to stop them, I was rethinking that trying-to-solve-this-on-my-own thing. I wanted to use my phone, but had no way to get to it.

"Why are you doing this?" I asked.

Hunter answered my question, surprising me. "It has to be done. But I told you before I didn't kill Juliana."

"Who killed her then? It had to be Victor," I said.

The smile on Victor's face was anything but friendly. "I wanted my money. If I had to kill Juliana to get it, so be it."

"In case you didn't realize, you can't get money back from a person after they're dead."

"I never knew the money was there," Juliana said.

"Plus, she didn't know the money was there," I conveyed her message.

"I told you he is the dimmest bulb in the chandelier," Charlotte said.

"So are you here to help Victor get the stolen money back?" I asked Hunter.

"I'm here to help myself. I want nothing to do with Victor."

"Don't you want to bring your girlfriend's murderer to justice?" I tried to remind him to do the right thing.

"Not at my expense." His words came out with impatience.

"What a snake," Charlotte said.

"That works out for me now, doesn't it," Victor said with that same evil smile.

"Shut up!" Hunter yelled at him.

"How could you do this? Don't help him," Juliana yelled.

Hunter's hand trembled and the gun moved downward. "I would never have hurt Juliana."

Yet he was ready to hurt us?

Hunter continued. "I didn't kill Juliana. Victor was looking for the stolen money."

"I knew you had the cash. I'd better get it back," Victor warned.

"So you were working together to get it back?" I asked.

"Both of them need to be in jail," Charlotte said.

Hunter motioned for us. It looked as if I wasn't getting out of this one. If only I had a chance to call Dylan.

"Ask him where he hid the money when he first took it," Juliana urged.

"Juliana wants to know what you did with the money after you took it? I know you didn't put it in the car right away."

Hunter looked at me for a moment and then he said, "I hid the stolen cash at my grandmother's home."

"You should be ashamed that you did that to your grandmother." Charlotte waved her finger at Hunter.

"Why would you do that? You put your grandmother at risk," I said.

He ran his hand through his hair. "I was in a hurry. Victor was coming for me. I did the first thing that came to mind." He motioned with the gun. "Now stop talking and get in my car."

"I wish he'd stop waving that thing around. Obviously, he doesn't know how to use the thing," Charlotte said.

"I didn't put my grandmother in danger. She can take care of herself," Hunter said.

"We went to visit her, you know?" I said.

"Yes, I'm aware. You're lucky you got out of there," Hunter said. "She was suspicious of both of you. She called me to come, but you left before I got there."

"What a sneaky grandmother," Heather said.

"I was suspicious of that woman." Irritation pinched between Charlotte's sculpted eyebrows.

That was the first I heard of it. Charlotte was just saying that now?

"Why hide it in the vintage stuff? Didn't you realize she would give it away?" I asked.

"I remembered a purse that she had with a secret

compartment inside. It was a perfect hiding spot for the money." Hunter opened his car door.

"I told you he doesn't think things through," Juliana said. "He was always doing things like that."

"Before I got back to retrieve the money, my grandmother had given the vintage items to Juliana."

"I bet that freaked him out," Charlotte said. "Serves him right."

"Your actions got Juliana killed," I said.

"I don't need you to remind me of that. You need to stop asking questions. This isn't an interview for the newspaper." Hunter waved the gun.

Just as we started to get in his car, Victor said, "Hunter drop the gun. You're not going anywhere until I get the money."

"What do you mean? I helped you. She was going to call the cops. Now you can get away," Hunter said.

"I'm getting away, but I'm doing it with the money. I know you still have the cash. I'm not falling for this story that the police have it," Victor said.

"But they do. I found it," I said.

"Shut up. I don't believe any of you. Now drop the gun before I shoot." He focused his weapon on Hunter.

Hunter slowly placed the gun on the ground and then held up his hands.

"This has more twists than a pretzel," Charlotte said.

"I told you I hid the money. Juliana had no idea stolen money was hidden in the purse my grandmother had given her." Hunter's hands remained high above his head.

"Drop the gun and put your hands up."

I recognized the voice right away.

"Thank goodness he's here," Charlotte said. "I could just kiss him."

I wasn't sure how Dylan had found us, but I was just thankful that he had. Victor placed the gun on the ground and then put his hands up.

"Are there any more guns?" Dylan asked as he moved by me.

I pointed. "There's one beside Hunter."

Dylan kept his gun focused on Hunter and Victor long enough to retrieve both guns then instructed the men to place their hands behind their heads and lean against Hunter's car.

Other police officers arrived and escorted Victor and Hunter to the police cruisers and placed them in the back seat.

I was glad Dylan didn't have to handle those guys alone any longer. Juliana had moved over to the car and was staring at Hunter. She was heartbroken that he had betrayed her love. I wished I could take away the feeling. Charlotte moved over to her and tried to comfort her. Heather and I stayed back so that we could talk to the police. They had a lot of questions for us.

"How did you know where to find me?" I asked Dylan when he walked over.

"I was driving by and just happened to spot your car parked over there. I thought I'd check on you and that was when I saw the scene," Dylan said.

"Oh, he was checking up on you. Cookie, you

could never hide from anyone in that car," Charlotte said.

This was one time when I was glad about that. "I'm glad you did," I said to Dylan.

"What brought you over here?" he asked.

I looked down at my shoes. I knew I wouldn't be able to avoid the question forever. "I saw Victor's car and I came to check it out."

Chapter 35

Cookie's Savvy Tips for Vintage Shopping

*With vintage clothing,
you can get a great quality piece
at a fraction of the cost of new.*

The next day we were at my shop. Well, except Juliana. She had moved on since she knew who'd murdered her. I was glad that she had been able to find peace, but of course I'd miss her. Charlotte wasn't going anywhere. She was giving me orders on which dress to put on the mannequin.

It was a bright day and a new start. I'd chosen to wear a late 1940s navy blue dress. The designer was unknown, but the dress was stunning. The pockets, collar, and cuffs were all cream-colored. The fabric had the same cream-colored polka dots. The fitted bodice showed off my curves. At least that was what Charlotte had said. The dress was truly gorgeous. For shoes I'd picked 1950s pumpkin orange patent leather peep-toe stiletto mules. The vamp was a shirred patent leather on one side and a corresponding side wrap to close the top. My handbag was a trendy spotted animal print with tortoiseshell Lucite handles. It added a bit of whimsy to my outfit. I was really into mixing patterns lately.

Charlotte was leaning against the counter. "You know something, Cookie? Why haven't you just asked the cat if she's your grandmother?"

"I did, and she didn't respond."

"Maybe she wasn't ready to talk then."

"I suppose, but I didn't think she was that fickle."

"Combine your grandmother with the cat and I think it's the most fickle thing on the planet."

She had a point there. "But like I said, Wind Song only talks when she's ready."

"You should try it again," Charlotte said.

Wind Song was pretending to sleep, watching us out of the corner of her eye.

I knew she was really listening. I felt her stare. "I suppose we could try again."

Wind Song closed her eyes.

"I don't know how easy it would be to get her to talk today. Besides, I feel ridiculous asking."

"Any more ridiculous than talking to ghosts and a cat you think is psychic?" Charlotte asked.

"No, I suppose not," I said. "How will I get her to talk?"

"Lure her over with some of those treats she likes so much."

I didn't think it would work, but I had to give it a

shot. First, I needed to retrieve the Ouija board from Heather's place.

"I'll be right back," I said, dashing for the door.

I made it over to her place and back in record time. I pulled out the bag and rattled it. Immediately Wind Song looked at me and jumped down from the window sill.

"Sometimes she's just too predictable," Charlotte said.

Wind Song jumped up onto the counter and I gave her a treat. "There are more where that came from, Wind Song. All you have to do is answer our questions."

I placed the Ouija board on the counter in front of her. Then I set the planchette where she could reach it easily. For good measure, I gave her another treat. She gobbled it up, then licked her paws.

I got right to it. "Wind Song, are you my Grandmother Pearl?"

"Maybe you shouldn't just ask it right away. You should ease into the question."

"It's a little too late now, isn't it, Charlotte? You should've told me that first."

"I didn't think I had to tell you everything."

Wind Song placed her paw on the planchette.

I watched her closely. "Here we go."

She was finally going to answer my question. I would know once and for all if Wing Song was my grandmother.

The bell over the door jingled, and Wind Song immediately moved her paw, as if she knew we wouldn't want to be caught. A customer entered and I knew we would have to wait. The woman walked across the floor, taking her time looking through each rack of clothing.

Normally, that would've made me happy, but I wanted her to get out of there so I could get my answer. I felt guilty. Finally, she left and didn't even buy anything.

"At least now we can get back to the question." I looked at Wind Song once again. "Are you my Grandmother Pearl?"

Wind Song reached out, placed her paw on the planchette again, and started moving it. My stomach did a dance. I knew where she was moving the planchette. *Yes* was on one side of the board, *no* on the other. The only reason she would be moving to the left side was if her answer was yes.

Sure enough, that was where she stopped. Charlotte and I gasped at the same time. I didn't hesitate to grab Wind Song in my arms and hug her tight. Then I plastered a few hundred kisses on her face too. I'd loved the cat before, but now even more.

"Oh, Grandma Pearl, are you okay?" Tears rolled down my cheeks.

"Get yourself together, Cookie. You're ruining your mascara."

I tried to compose myself and placed Wind Song back on the counter. Should I call her Grandma Pearl? I was happy and sad at the same time. I had to do something to help her. I couldn't let my grandmother be stuck in this dimension as a cat when she needed to move on.

"How did this happen?" I said.

"I think we know how it happened," Charlotte said. "Cookie, I'm so happy for you."

I knew it looked as if I wasn't happy—I had tears in my eyes—but I was. Seeing my grandmother again was the best feeling. But if my grandmother was inside of the cat, where was the cat's spirit? I had so many questions. "Wind Song, er, Grandma Pearl, where is the cat's spirit?"

She placed her furry paw on the planchette and moved around to the letters. Finally, she spelled out that the cat was with her inside the body.

No wonder she liked that tuna delight so much. "Don't worry, Grandma Pearl. I'll help you."

"Why are you talking so loudly, Cookie?" Charlotte asked.

"Well, Grandma Pearl was hard of hearing before she passed on."

"I think you're hurting the cat's ears. You might want to turn it down a notch," Charlotte said.

The cat started moving the planchette around the board again. She was saying something else. The next thing I knew, she had spelled out that she wanted to stay.

"Do you enjoy being a cat?" I asked.

That question didn't receive a response.

"Cookie, don't ask ridiculous questions," Charlotte said.

I checked the time. "Isn't it time for you to meet Sam?"

"I still have thirty minutes."

"I didn't know there was time in the other dimension."

Charlotte checked her gold Rolex watch. "Well,

there's time here isn't there? I told him I had to help you."

"Lucky me," I said.

"You are too sassy." She placed her hands on her hips.

"I got it from my grandmother."

Wind Song meowed.

The door opened and Dylan walked in. He tossed his hand up in a wave.

"He seems awfully happy today," Charlotte said.

"Good morning." After placing a box on the counter, he leaned forward and in one smooth movement covered my mouth with his. His mouth was strong, but his lips gentle.

"True romance," Charlotte said as she watched us.

I could do without the audience. "What's in the box?"

"It's for you. Open it up." He motioned.

"Oh, a present. I love gifts." Charlotte hurried over.

I quirked an eyebrow.

"Go ahead." He motioned again.

Even after opening the top, the box was too tall for me to see inside. I stretched up on my tiptoes, pulled the box a little closer, and peered over the edge. The vintage items that Hunter's grandmother had given Juliana filled the box. Without thinking, a squeal of delight escaped my lips. All the items were there. Even the turquoise hat that everyone had wanted because either they thought it was worth a lot of money or they thought money was hidden inside.

I looked at Dylan. "Why did you bring this?"

"The stuff is yours now," he said with a smile.

"Are you serious? Why?" I asked as I took out one of the sweaters. It felt like Christmas morning.

"The stuff is gorgeous," Charlotte said.

"Juliana's family wanted you to have it. They are so thankful for your part in capturing Juliana's murderer."

"I don't know what to say."

"Just say thank you," Dylan said.

"Send them a thank-you card," Charlotte said.

I sorted through the items. "As much as I would love to keep them, I don't think I should."

"Why not?" Charlotte and Dylan asked at the same time.

"Who should have them?" Dylan quirked an eyebrow.

"I want to give them back to Hunter's grand-mother."

Dylan shook his head. "That's not possible."

"It's not?"

"Nope," Dylan said.

"Why not?" I asked.

"We had to arrest her too. She was part of the scheme to steal the money in the first place."

"What about Aunt Regina?"

"She'll be charged for her part in teaming up with Hunter and Victor."

"I knew it!" Charlotte said.

I wanted to laugh at her reaction but didn't. I simply looked at Dylan and smiled.

Acknowledgments

*I'd like to thank my editor Michaela Hamilton
and my agent Jill Marsal.
Much love to both!*

Don't miss the ghostly fun
in the next Haunted Vintage mystery

IF THE HAUNTING FITS, WEAR IT

Coming soon from Kensington Publishing Corp.

Keep reading to enjoy an excerpt . . .

Chapter 1

"Come one step closer and I'll kill you," I said.

The giant black hairy spider didn't listen as he scurried toward me. I ran in the opposite direction. The creature was the size of a rat and probably would have survived any attempts to extinguish it. The best option for me was to let him run off into the little dark corner he came from. I'd grab what I came into the attic for and we'd both be happy. We'd call a truce and just leave each other alone.

Running a vintage clothing shop was not without its hazards—such as the aforementioned spider . . . and mice. That was what I got when I crawled around old places looking for treasures. Vintage clothing was my thing. When I spotted a circle skirt, a great pair of pedal pushers, or a fabulous pair of wedge heels, my heart skipped a beat. A vintage discovery truly was an adrenaline rush. I'd turned my passion into a career when I opened It's Vintage Y'all, my little boutique in the charming small town of Sugar Creek, Georgia.

I wore a 1950s Ruth Starling flower patterned dress. It had tiny rhinestone buttons down the front, a full skirt, and a darted waistline. Perfect for spring, the dress was the bee's knees. On my feet I wore pale yellow wedge heels with a small bow across the vamp. Wedges were my favorite and the color brought out the buttery gerbera daisies in the dress.

An ad for vintage clothing for sale had led me to this old attic. At least it had a small window on the other side of the room, allowing a small amount of daylight to seep inside. It was a typical attic with exposed beams, cobwebs, and stacks of boxes. An old dress form stood in the left corner by the window. Every time I glanced up, I thought the thing was a person staring at me. Maybe that explained the creepy feeling I had.

I'd been told quite a few great vintage pieces were stored in the old trunk located in the middle of the cramped space. The new owner had found the items when she'd bought the house and said I could just take whatever I wanted. The words were like magic to my ears. I was willing to deal with almost anything for free vintage, even fighting a bear . . . or a bear-sized spider. Mostly, I was looking for hats.

The trunk groaned as I opened the lid. Layers of dust whirled to life. My eyes widened when I spotted the red 1940s boater hat. It had a narrow brim with a small red veil. Perched on the edge of the brim was a velvet flocked bird with feathers in matching red hues. I was in hat heaven. As I sifted through the trunk I found more treasures. There must have been at least twenty hats, all equally fabulous.

When I looked up from the old truck, I gasped and fell back onto my butt. A sixty-something woman was standing in the corner of the room, her stare locked on me. She wore a black silk crepe mid-length dress. On her hands were delicate white gloves. Discreet pearl drops dotted her ears and a matching necklace encircled her neck. The 1940s tilt hat was made of black cellophane straw, the crown encircled with black grosgrain ribbon. She completed her outfit with simple black pumps and a matching pocketbook.

I found it odd that her hat looked so much like the ones in the trunk. Had she taken one of them? I hadn't heard her enter the room. Maybe I'd been so consumed by the finds that I didn't notice. Had she been there all along? On my feet again, I stood behind the trunk with the hats still in my arms. Since the woman's frown sent a clear message that she wasn't happy to see me, I used the trunk as my shield. It created a nice barrier between us.

"What do you think you're doing?" she demanded.

Before I could answer, another voice chimed in. "Cookie Chanel, come down from there. I'm not going in. I don't want to get my outfit dirty. Besides, I may be a ghost, but I'm not going in that spooky place."

It was not the time to deal with Charlotte Meadows. She was a ghost that refused to leave my side. Ever since I found her at an estate sale, she'd been stuck on me like flies on honey. She'd been attached to her killer wardrobe, but now she was affixed to me.

I looked at the corner again. The black-clad woman wasn't there. "Where'd you go?"

I looked to the other side of the room. She was there. Was she playing games with me?

I focused my attention on her so she couldn't get away. "I'm sorry, but the woman downstairs said these hats were available."

She shifted the pocketbook from her right arm to her left. "They're my hats and they're not available."

That was a bummer. I started to put the hats back in the trunk, but I noticed something odd. The lower half of the woman was completely see-through. Why hadn't I noticed that sooner? The longer I looked at her, the more solid she became.

Unfortunately, I knew exactly what that meant. *Oh no, not again.* Why did it happen to me? I enjoyed helping the ghosts, but it confused me. Why *me*?

I had to let this woman know she was no longer in this dimension. Were the items in the trunk hers? Considering the gorgeous outfit she wore, I'd be willing to bet that was the case. I could understand why she was so concerned about the things in the trunk.

I picked up a hat. A ghost wouldn't keep me from taking what had been offered. "You do realize that you are a ghost?" I asked as I filled my arms with the hats again.

She glared at me and said, "Well, that's neither here nor there. They're my hats."

So she did know she was a ghost.

Charlotte poked her head through the door. Literally. "What seems to be the problem, Cookie?

Hurry it up. I don't want to have to come all the way in there."

Before I even answered, she spotted the woman across the room. Suddenly, Charlotte had no problem with setting foot in the attic. She popped in and stood beside me with her arms crossed in front of her chest. She was pretty territorial about me, as if I were her own personal psychic. Charlotte was dressed in a white tailored pant suit and a beige silk tank that peeked out from under her jacket. On her feet, she wore nude-colored Christian Louboutins with five-inch heels. One perk of being a spirit was Charlotte got to wear whatever outfit she thought up in her mind.

She tapped her foot against the floor. "And who is this?"

"Not that it's any of your concern, my name is Maureen Weber." She stared at Charlotte. "Who are you?"

"I'm Charlotte Meadows. That's all you need to know."

I could see this was getting us nowhere. "Maureen, I understand you're attached to your hats, but since you no longer need them, maybe I could let someone else use them? Someone who would really enjoy them." I forced a smile onto my face.

"So you want to steal my hats."

Charlotte shook her fist. "Don't call Cookie a thief."

I clapped my hands. "Ladies, ladies. Let's not argue, shall we?"

What could I do to get this woman to let me have the hats? I suppose I would just have to leave them in the trunk. That made me sad. I was on a mission to find fantastic hats for a very special event. Danielle Elston had requested a vintage hat to wear for the upcoming Kentucky Derby. She simply couldn't go to the derby without a fantastic hat. Danielle had the money to buy any hat she wanted and had requested that I help her.

Finally solid, Maureen moved a couple steps closer and pointed at Charlotte. "I know she's a ghost, but something seems different about you. I think you're still with the living." She sashayed over to us.

Charlotte rolled her eyes. "Good heavens. It looks like two pigs fighting in a sack. One says you let me go by this time and I'll let you go by the next."

"Charlotte! That's not very nice," I said.

Maureen looked me up and down. "So if you're living, how can you see me?"

I exchanged a look with Charlotte. "I don't really know how I can see you."

A look of happiness spread across Maureen's face. "Since you can see me, you can help find my murderer."